I0699349

Other books by Deirdre Hutchins

The Paranormal Investigators League series

PIL #1 Voodoo in Savannah

PIL #2 A Hanging in Tucson

PIL #3 Suicide on Sunset

PIL #4 The Legend of Providence

PIL #5 Darkness in Denver

PIL #6 Spirits in Seattle

PIL Prequel: The Origin Story

The Dark Prophecy trilogy

1: Resurrection of the Vampire

2: Vengeance of the Damned

3: Deliverance from the Prophecy

The Daphne Winters Psychic Investigation Series

DW1 The Body and the Soul

DW2 Finding Maddy

DW3 Dropped Dead

These are all available from the San Joaquin Valley Press.

Visit us at www.sanjoaquinvalleypress.com

Daphne Winters Psychic Investigation Series
#4

Vanished

A Novel

By Deirdre Hutchins

San Joaquin Valley Press
Fresno, California

Vanished is published by
        San Joaquin Valley Press
        P.O. Box 9485
        Fresno, CA 93792
        www.sanjoaquinvalleypress.com

Cover design by Andria Davis Kaye
The cover is a collage of elements from Shutterstock:
445029169 Portrait of a sad curly girl by Cookie Studios and
2526475773 Sacramento park by Slog Photography

ISBN 979-8-9905729-2-8

PROLOGUE

Forty years is a long time to be missing.

I wander the streets. I lurk in shadows. I try to reach out to my family but I only instill fear and panic instead of comfort.

I am so alone. So utterly alone.

Every night I cry softly into the void of eternity, hoping that someone hears my torment, hoping that someone is actually still looking for me. But how? How after forty years can my story actually be told? How can I finally get justice?

I know where my body is, decayed as it is after all these years. And I know who is to blame.

All I need is a chance to lead them there. All I need is for someone to listen.

On the darkest nights, the ones where the moonlight is masked by clouds and even shadows dare not make an appearance, I could almost lose hope. My despair is so overwhelming.

But I push on. Because I cannot rest—will not rest—until my story is told. I cry. I despair. I wallow in my solitude. But through it all, I never give up hope.

I'll never stop believing that my truth will one day be told.

1.

"Let's start with what we do know." Miguel, Gina and Sheffley sat around a conference table with every paper from the Melissa Amber Daniel file.

"She was taking classes at Fresno State. I have her enrollment and course schedule here." Gina held up the document that substantiated this fact as if anyone questioned Amber's status as a student.

"Last seen leaving her apartment for work on Wednesday, January 4, 1989, at four p.m., but she's not reported missing for three days." Sheffley looked up as the timeframe dawned on him as bizarre. "No one missed her for three days?"

"That's a good question, Sheffley. Write it down," Miguel instructed. "So her roommate says good-bye without a worry in the world, but she never shows up for work and no one says a thing to authorities until her mother reports her missing on January seventh. That's definitely a gap."

"Where did she work again?" Gina asked, leaning over the table to find the document that would answer her question.

"The Denny's on Shaw, near Fashion Fair." Miguel knew this fact by heart.

"Whoever her shift manager was, we need to interview that person," Gina continued, still rummaging through the papers looking for answers.

"His name is Alex Milton and he was interviewed back in 1989." Miguel stood and quickly found the interview notes. "He pretty much knew nothing. Just said she didn't show up for work so he had to call another waitress to cover her shift. And he was fairly annoyed about it."

"Servers." Gina rolled her eyes. "We don't say waitress anymore."

Miguel raised an eyebrow. "I'm reading the notes from 1989. Cut me some slack. Times were different."

"And nothing is ever found of her?" Sheffley asked skeptically.

"They found her car covered in blood, but no purse. No wallet. And no Melissa Amber Daniel." Miguel frowned at the prospect of what that meant as he rummaged through the papers in search of the photo of her car. "Red Mazda coupe. Presumed abandoned by the perp."

"She just vanished." Gina almost whispered the words. If she wasn't a homicide detective, she wouldn't believe it was even possible for someone to completely disappear. But in her profession, she'd seen a lot of horrific things. It solidified her belief in the depravity of humanity.

"Was there ever a list of persons of interest? Any potential suspects identified?" Sheffley asked. He knew no self-respecting homicide detective would just let a case get cold without working it until their muscles ached and their heads hurt.

Miguel shook his head. "Nothing substantive. She had a boyfriend, but he had a rock-solid alibi for the night she went missing."

"Which was?" It was Gina's turn to raise an eyebrow. In her experience, random acts of violence were rare. Her victims usually fell prey to someone close to them in their lives. Like a boyfriend.

"He was a local DJ. Michael Benton, but his stage name was DJ Bendy." Miguel tossed another paper across the table to Gina. "He was working a gig that night and multiple witnesses were able to corroborate."

"We should re-interview him. And the roommate. And bring Daphne along. You know there are some things that just don't quite translate to a police report," Gina stated.

"I know you guys love me." Daphne waltzed into the room with a flourish that only she could muster, reacting to hearing her name moments before. A swirl of energy just followed her everywhere. She carried two bags of food and dropped them unceremoniously on the center of the conference table. "Here. I brought you all tacos."

"I love your psychic girlfriend, Miguel." Sheffley wasted no time in tearing into the bags of food. "I was craving tacos."

"My talents do go beyond helping ghosts." Daphne smiled with pure self-satisfaction.

Miguel shook his head before leaning in to kiss Daphne's cheek. "Thanks for the tacos, Daph."

"Hi, Daphne. I was talking about you because something doesn't let me trust that boyfriend." Gina frowned. The smell of tacos alone couldn't sway her from the mission of discovering what happened to Amber.

"Are we talking about the DJ? Or the professor?" Daphne asked casually as she dug through the bags to grab a tortilla chip and pop it in her mouth with a loud crunch.

The detectives all froze.

"I'm sorry. The what?" Miguel shuffled pages all around the table. Granted he hadn't had the chance to read every single paper, but he knew the contents better than anyone else in the room. "There was no mention of any professor."

"Huh." Daphne shrugged. "Well, maybe she hid that relationship pretty well. But she was sleeping with her history professor. Something with a K. Dr. Kent. Dr. Kelvin. Dr. Kensington. No. That one has too many syllables."

"I'm sure we can get the name from Fresno State." Miguel looked at Sheffley and the young investigator correctly interpreted it as an instruction.

"A secret affair with a college professor is certainly a new twist investigators didn't know about in the eighties." Gina pursed her lips. Yes, she wanted to make headway on the case, but the thought of all the possibilities of what could have happened to the young college girl running through Gina's mind was still sobering, at best.

"A new twist indeed." Miguel looked from Gina to Sheffley before settling his eyes on the beautiful blonde psychic with the disheveled hair. "And it's a potential motive for murder."

2.

Professor Stephen Kelly closed the blinds to his front window and withdrew to the kitchen in the back of his house. He put the kettle on and prepared his afternoon tea just as he had for the large majority of his eighty years on this planet.

He had seen the nondescript car out front and knew precisely what it meant. After all these years they were going to ask about Amber.

And he found that he simply couldn't care enough to run.

Forty years ago he had waited with a pit in his stomach, anticipation building over the affair he had had with a woman twenty years his junior. He assumed the police would put all the pieces together and come ask him about their relationship.

But they never did.

He continued teaching at Fresno State just as he always had. He stayed married to Pamela. And Amber was never seen again.

He had dodged a bullet then and he knew it. But now the question remained. How forthright should he be with the detectives?

The tea kettle screamed in response to his thoughts, giving him a moment of pause as he poured. He blew gently before taking a small sip.

Let them ask whatever they may. He didn't owe anyone anything. What happened with Amber was buried now with her.

And that's exactly where it would stay.

3.

"I'm sitting right outside his house," Sheffley told Miguel. He flipped his phone to his other ear and leaned his weight against the car door. "And get this. No one at Fresno State had any clue about his relationship with Amber. Apparently, Professor Kelly was considered the quintessential family man."

Miguel huffed into the phone, a sound that crossed an exasperated sigh with a laugh at how often people turned out to be nothing like the mask they used to fool the world. "Why am I not surprised?"

"Want me to wait for Daphne?" Sheffley asked.

"Yeah. She and Gina will be there in five."

"And where are you?" It was simple curiosity. No judgment.

"I'm pulling in front of the surprisingly

magnificent home of the former DJ Bendy." Miguel parked his car in front of a large brick home that reminded Miguel of an apartment building. "Wonder what this guy did with his life to turn it around so much."

"Or who he's extorting." Sheffley couldn't resist the comment. It was as natural for him to assume criminal activity as it was for him to drink water. He cringed at his own crassness, but then let it go when Miguel began laughing.

"Well. I hope you're kidding. If it turns out he's profiting from Amber's death, I will greatly enjoy arresting him." Miguel climbed out of his car and slammed his door as loudly as he could. He liked to give potential interviewees a little reason to peek out their window and watch him walk up. "I'll see what this guy knows while you find out what the professor knows. Someone must have seen something. We just have to find them."

With barely a good-bye, Miguel and Sheffley ended their call, and Miguel rapped on Michael Benton's front door.

A beautiful middle-aged woman answered the door, her long dark hair pulled over one shoulder. "May I help you?" She smiled warmly and it seemed sincere.

"Oh." For some reason this caught Miguel off guard. He was so used to people being annoyed by his visits that her welcoming was jarring. "Detective Miguel Alvaraz, ma'am. Hoping to ask a few questions of a Mike Benton."

Miguel pulled his badge out of his pocket, but the woman barely even looked at it before she was opening the door widely.

"Detective. Please come in. Mike is upstairs." The woman gestured for Miguel to follow her into the home. He felt swallowed by the house as he entered the largest foyer he had ever seen in a building that wasn't a hotel. "I'm Sheila, by the way," the woman added. "Mike's wife."

"Nice to meet you." Miguel nodded at Sheila, truly happy to know who she was and her relation to his person of interest.

Sheila led him to a large family room with exposed wood beams and a fireplace the size of Miguel's current apartment. "You can have a seat here. I'll go get Mike."

Once Sheila Benton had left the room, Miguel began snooping around. He enjoyed doing this whenever he had the chance. He found it told him so much about the person, things they may not ever say openly once the topic of murder came up. Funny how that made people clam right up.

As expected, there were photos of a young DJ Bendy with several important-seeming people, but no one Miguel recognized. He was clearly working events in prestigious places, at least back in his younger days.

A wooden hutch housed a collection of family photos, ranging from weddings to graduations to good old-fashioned posed family pictures where everyone wears the obligatory matching outfit. Miguel stifled a laugh because never in a million years could he imagine his mother dressing the Alvarez family alike for a professional photo session.

A gold record hung on the wall with Mike's name and a song called "Forever more." Again, Miguel was completely at a loss as to exactly what the song was that had taken local small-town DJ to star status.

"I was a music producer on that album," Michael Benton explained as he entered the room, catching Miguel looking far too closely at the gold record. "My biggest crowning achievement."

He smiled as warmly as his wife had. No malice. And seemingly no nerves about a police detective in his home. These were not the types of people who were used to being on the wrong end of a police investigation.

"Congratulations, Mr. Benton. That must have been quite the project." Miguel followed Mike's lead and sat on the oversized white sectional.

"It was. One of the highlights of my life. Besides my family. Fulfillment of a lifelong dream to work in music." He leaned back casually, both arms wrapped around the back of the couch. "So, what brings you by? How can I help, detective?"

Miguel leaned in, elbows resting on his knees. "I'm here about a missing persons cold case. Melissa Amber Daniel. Does the name ring a bell?"

Mike instantly frowned. "There's a name I haven't heard in years." He rubbed his chin thoughtfully. "But not a day goes by where she doesn't cross my mind at least once."

"How so?" Miguel watched the DJ-turned-music-producer carefully, looking for signs of nervousness or discomfort or untruths. But if the man was going to ramble, Miguel was going to let him.

"She was my first love. And I go to a gig, and then I never see her again. It destroyed me." Mike's eyes were laden with sadness. It seemed sincere. "I never knew what happened to her. Never even got to say good-bye." He shook his head. "She just disappeared from my life. From everyone's life. How does that happen?"

Miguel could sense someone who struggled with closure. He saw this a lot with families of victims, especially of ones who never got answers. They retain a hope against all odds that wars constantly with the truths their brain is telling them. Without a body, they simply can't stop believing that she will one day walk back through the door.

"So, when exactly was the last time you saw Amber?" Miguel prodded.

Mike rubbed his chin. "Earlier that day. I came by her house to hang with her a bit. We both had to work that night, so we didn't want to miss any time together during the day."

This was corroborated by the police report. At the very least DJ Bendy's story hadn't changed in forty years.

"When did you realize she was missing?" Miguel wanted to see what he could find out about why no one worried for three days.

"I called her the next day, but Maggie said she

wasn't home."

"Maggie the roommate?" Miguel clarified.

Mike nodded. "Yeah. I didn't worry too much at that time because she was a busy college student. It wasn't unusual for her to meet up with friends at the library or something for a project. What *was* weird was when she never called me back. Amber and I rarely went more than a day without seeing each other if we could help it."

"What did you do when she didn't call you back?"

"I called and talked to Maggie a few more times and then I got really worried. A couple days later I called Amber's mom and asked her if she'd seen Amber." The lines on Mike's face got deeper as he relived the painful event from his past.

"And she hadn't, I assume."

Mike took a deep breath. "She hadn't. And then we both began to get very worried. We started calling everyone we knew. Friends, family. I called Amber's boss. We called hospitals. No one knew anything."

"What did Maggie the roommate think about all this? She never worried?" Miguel asked. It seemed strange to him that the first person who should have realized something was wrong had acted so flippantly, according to Mike's story.

"Ugh. She was such a bitch. Never once acted like she knew or cared what happened to Amber." Mike shook his head. "I never liked that lady."

"Why did they live together then?" Miguel had to ask. He'd assumed they were at least somewhat friendly with one another.

Mike shrugged. "Cheaper rent. They were both English majors at Fresno State. I think it was just convenience."

"Do you know of anyone who might want to hurt Amber?" Miguel fished out his notebook, hoping he might learn something new.

Mike Benton stood up and walked over to the hutch with the family photos Miguel had been looking at moments before. He didn't look dismissive of the question. He was pensive, remembering a different time in his life. "The path I had been on at that phase of my life was so different than the journey I ended up taking." He picked up the photo of his wife. "I would've married Amber if I could have. I would've lived a quiet life providing for her as she taught kids how to read and write. That was her dream. To be a teacher." He smiled warmly at Miguel. "But that dream was blown to bits when Amber went missing." He placed the photo of his wife back down and walked back to Miguel. "No, she had no enemies. If I had had any inkling of a clue who I thought did this, they'd be dead right now."

It was a promise, not a threat. Time had healed the wound just enough to allow him to say the words with no emotion, but not to take away the sheer confidence that he would've done it back in 1989.

"And if we find her alive?" Miguel had to ask.

Mike smiled, a warm smile that lit up his eyes. "I've lived a good life in spite of it all. But if we find Amber and she's happy and healthy, nothing in this world could make me happier. It's all I ever wanted. To find her and know she's okay."

"Just one more question, Mr. Benton." Miguel continued taking notes. "Do you know anything about a professor named Stephen Kelly?"

A deep crease formed across the former DJ's face as the name took him way back in time. "You mean the douchebag history professor?"

"Uh, yes, he teaches history." Miguel waited for more explanation on the colorful way to describe Amber's secret amour.

"I know he was a complete jerk. No one liked him." As all the pieces slid into place, Mike became suddenly inquisitive. "What does that have to do with Amber?"

Miguel chose to keep his cards close to his chest, lest the emotions force a large shift in this line of questioning. "Why did no one like him? Do you have specific examples?"

Mike frowned as he struggled to remember

conversations from so many years before. "Nothing specific. Just I remember Amber and Maggie constantly complaining that he was unfair, picked on people. That kind of thing."

"So they didn't like him?"

"Not at all. I got the sense that he was one of the least liked professors at Fresno State back in the day." Mike laughed at the memory. "There was no social media, of course, so I can only go by what my friends all said."

"Did you take any of his classes or have any personal experiences?"

"No. I didn't go to Fresno State. I can only tell you what Amber told me."

Miguel shifted a bit in his seat. He hated to go there, but he had to probe, had to see how Mike Benton reacted to word about his former girlfriend's relationship. If he knew, it could be a strong motive. If he didn't know, his world would shatter. "And did Amber ever share any positive feelings? Like maybe she found him attractive?"

Mike looked shocked to his core and the reaction seemed genuine. "No way. He was just a professor she didn't like. I got the sense she liked nothing about him."

"So, if someone were to accuse her of having a secret relationship with Professor Kelly, you would…?" Miguel prompted.

But Mike Benton shook his head, sticking to his guns. "That's absolutely ridiculous. If anyone said that, then they didn't know Amber at all."

"Well, thank you for your time, Mr. Benton. If you think of anything at all, the smallest little thing could be the biggest help." Miguel stood up and stuck his notebook in his shirt pocket.

"Do you know if they ever found her necklace?" Mike asked, his chin jutting out like it was the one question *he* had in this interview.

Miguel froze. There was nothing in any police reports about a necklace. "No, they haven't. But if you give me some details I can poke around."

"It was a diamond necklace from her

grandmother. She always wore it everywhere. It was her prized possession, but for some reason she didn't wear it to work that night which was very unlike her."

"But you didn't see her before she left for work, so how do you know?" Miguel asked.

"Maggie told me. And then a couple days later when she was officially reported missing, Mrs. Daniels asked for the necklace back, but it was nowhere to be found." Mike Benton shook his head. "I always figured that was connected somehow."

Interesting indeed. But most intriguing was the way this roommate kept popping up in not so glamorous a light. "I'll keep an eye out for word of it. Thank you, Mr. Benton."

Miguel extended his hand and Mike Benton shook it warmly.

After Miguel had let himself out, Sheila Benton was confident enough to walk back into the room. "Was that about Amber?" Standing behind him, she rested her chin on her husband's shoulder.

"Yeah. Looks like they're going to finally get us some answers after all these years." Mike couldn't look at his wife. She knew everything, of course she did. But Amber had a way of being a third party in this relationship that always made things awkward. Although Sheila never appeared to be upset by it.

"That will be nice for everyone to have closure." She wrapped her arms around her husband's waist. Despite it all, she knew this was a great source of pain for him.

He huffed a small laugh. "Someone told the detective that Amber had feelings for her history professor."

"Oh?" This caught Sheila's attention. "Do you think it could be true?"

Mike shook his head. "Maybe everything I ever believed was all a lie. But if it is true, then that asshole for sure knows something."

4.

"I saw him close the blinds, but he's in there." Sheffley caught Gina and Daphne up to speed the second they climbed out of Gina's car.

Gina had to look at Daphne before asking Sheffley, "So he saw you and closed the blinds? Like he's trying to hide?"

Sheffley shrugged. "I don't know why, but he did."

Gina rolled her eyes. "If he runs, I'm going to whip up a reason to arrest him."

"Nah, he's in there," Daphne answered. "He just doesn't want to face his demons."

"People who abuse power never do." Gina rapped on the door with three hard knocks. Silence greeted them.

After what felt like forever, Sheffley pounded on the door and shouted, "Police. Open up."

They heard a slight shuffle on the other side of the door and then the sound of several locks sliding back. The man that greeted them had been weathered by time. He was still tall and handsome, but with an abundance of lines accenting his face and hair that had long since given way to the salty side of salt and pepper.

"How can I help you?" the older gentleman asked, his voice calm and smooth, like a radio disc jockey. He must have been great at lectures.

Gina flashed her badge and took the lead. "Detective Gina Malone, Fresno P.D. Cold Case division. Professor Stephen Kelly?" She continued after his slight nod of affirmation. "We just have a few questions for you about a former student of yours."

"Amber Daniels, I assume?" he asked, still as cool as a cucumber.

"Sure nailed that one right out the gate," Sheffley muttered.

Professor Kelly only turned his head a millimeter in Sheffley's direction before responding. "Well, it's an easy matter of deductive reasoning. I only ever had one student go missing whereby a cold case detective might be asking me questions. This isn't rocket science, detective."

"May we come in and ask a few things?" Gina said, ignoring the interchange between Sheffley and their person of interest. She had a case to solve.

"No, you may not. I don't know enough to warrant you coming into my home." His voice was barely above a whisper, controlled as he was. Too controlled in a way. It was eerie and weird. Gina had to fight the chill that washed over her.

"Very well." Gina barely resisted rolling her eyes, but she'd had interviews on the porch before and she really couldn't care less. If she needed to get into the Kelly home, she could come back with a warrant. "Can you describe your relationship with Ms. Daniels?"

"Of course. She was a student in my history 101

class. And she wasn't even a very bright history student. Just an average member of my class. She only stands out, sad to say, because of what happened to her."

"Outside of class, did she ever come to office hours or seek private tutoring or anything?" Gina asked.

Professor Kelly folded his arms across his chest and leaned against the doorway that he continued blocking from the investigators. "No. Not that I recall."

Gina stole a side-eyed glance at Daphne who was remaining strangely deadpan. So she continued. "Can you respond to the rumor that you may have had a personal relationship with Ms. Daniels?"

Professor Kelly's face blanched, but only for a second before re-establishing his veneer of a cold, distant old man. "Detective Malone. I had hundreds of students every semester and I taught for over forty years. Every once in a while, a student became enamored with me. It happens."

"I understand, but how many of those enamored students also end up missing with foul play suspected?"

Gina let that one simmer for a moment before stating, "I'm going to need your complete whereabouts for January 4, 1989."

The professor scoffed. "I can hardly remember last week, let alone what I was doing forty years ago."

"You were with her," Daphne blurted. And then Gina smiled. There was the Daphne she knew and loved. Daphne held up a hand and closed her eyes as she read the truth. "You were in her passenger seat. Maybe she drove you somewhere? And that was January 4, 1989."

"Preposterous. I never rode with her anywhere as a passenger in her car." Professor Kelly at least had the decency to look completely shocked.

"Daphne here is a psychic medium, and she's rarely wrong, if ever," Gina explained. "So do you want to maybe take a moment to think back why you might have been in Amber's car the day she went missing?"

He remembered. It was written all over his face. But he took a moment to consider how much to admit. "All right. I'll come clean." The moment he said the words, a weight lifted off his chest. He had borne it for so long that he couldn't even remember a time when the knot wasn't lumped in his throat and threatening to drag him under.

"Thank you," Gina acknowledged.

Professor Kelly sighed and his shoulders slumped. His mask of coolness slipped right off like it was adhered with butter. "Amber was far from the only student I'd had a relationship with. But you have to understand, I had a wife and family. I had so much to lose."

Gina nodded. "I understand why you'd be hesitant to share this detail. But if you have any information about our case…"

"Amber was blackmailing me that day," Professor Kelly said far too quickly.

Gina looked questioningly at Daphne, who, equally curious, responded, "He's telling the truth."

"Okay, Mr. Kelly. I believe you," Gina answered. "Blackmailing you about the relationship?"

He nodded and swallowed hard. "She threatened

to go to my wife and to tell the university. I begged her, pleaded with her for discretion."

"So, she refused to comply and you attacked her? Or what?" Gina prodded.

"No, not at all." He looked at the ground, the shame of his selfishness all those years ago finally catching up to him. "We came to an agreement and I left. That's the honest truth."

"An agreement about what?" Sheffley had to ask.

"Amber was in love with me and I did not return the affection. She wanted to continue the relationship beyond the semester. And so I agreed to continue seeing her so that she didn't tell my wife."

"You understand that her blackmailing you right before she goes missing is highly suspicious, right?" Gina asked, eyebrow raised.

Professor Kelly turned to Daphne, a pleading in his eyes. "But then I left. I promised not to end things and then got in my car and left. That's the truth. I swear."

Daphne squinted as she listened to Professor Kelly. Then she turned her head to one side and said, "I don't like you."

"It's the honest-to-God truth. When I left, she was sitting in her car about to head to work. Perfectly fine." Professor Kelly looked from Gina to Sheffley and then back to Daphne.

"Was the car moving while you had this convo? Or where did it take place exactly?" Gina asked.

"In the parking lot in front of her apartments on Shaw." Professor Kelly fidgeted with his hands, nervously begging that someone believe his story now that he was finally telling it. "She was about to leave for work, and I hopped in her passenger seat to tell her we couldn't continue our relationship. I was worried about my marriage and reputation. She didn't drive off until after I left. I swear."

"And did you see her actually pull away?" Sheffley asked.

"Well. No. I drove off first. I assume she was

right behind me."

"You abused your position of authority to prey on young women. It's distasteful." Daphne dropped her judgment like a gavel. And then she turned to Gina. "As much as I hate this guy, he didn't kill Amber. He's telling the truth."

The relief the professor felt rolled off his shoulders as he let the tension fall.

"If she believes you, I believe you." Gina indicated to Daphne as she spoke to the professor. "But you are one of the last people to see Amber Daniels alive. Why have you stayed silent all these years?"

Professor Stephen Kelly said nothing, but he glanced at Daphne for the reprieve. Someone to save him from the embarrassment of having to say the words out loud.

"Because he's a selfish prick." Daphne snorted. "He didn't want anyone to know about his extracurricular activities, lest he be shunned from the world of academia." She glared at Amber's former lover with piercing eyes. "Because *that's* more important than someone's actual life."

"Did anyone at all know about your affair with Amber? Someone who might have had a reason to be jealous? Like her boyfriend, perhaps?" Gina asked.

Professor Kelly shook his head. "She wasn't seeing anyone but me and my wife has never found out. And I hope she never does." He said it in a way that suggested he was asking for the detectives to be discreet. They had no intention of complying with that wish. In their line of work, they couldn't tiptoe around various transgressions.

You're on your own in the world of crime and punishment.

But Gina did sneak a glance over at Daphne, who simply shrugged in reply. She had to hand it to Amber. The girl sure had her secrets.

"So who, in your mind, might have wanted to hurt her, Mr. Kelly?" Gina had to ask.

In a flash it all became very clear to Daphne, like

a magnifying glass suddenly coming into focus. Professor Kelly had spent forty years worrying about his own hide. He had never once spared a thought about what had happened to the young girl whose heart he had toyed with. Missing, possibly dead. And all he cared about was his own reputation and status.

"I... I didn't really know her. Stolen kisses. Hidden rendezvous. But intimate life details..." He shook his head. "We never shared those."

"So you don't have a theory at all?" Gina kept probing. "Didn't see someone suspicious in the parking lot, or remember someone obsessed with her? Nothing?"

But it was Daphne who answered for the professor again. "You're wasting your time here, Gina. He was just her secret lover. Nothing more."

His face said that he agreed, but he wisely kept his mouth shut.

"Then I guess we're done for now, Mr. Kelly." Gina smiled the most predatory smile Daphne had ever seen on her beautiful face. "But we're going to find out what happened to Amber. And if I find out that you could have saved her years ago if you had just come forward… I'm going to really enjoy watching your life fall apart when the truth comes out."

"I've never claimed to be perfect, Detective Malone." The old man's radio voice was back, calm and collected. "But I absolutely do hope you find her. I've never wished her any ill will."

"Of course not," Daphne said. It was people like this that made her prefer the company of ghosts. "Because that would mean you had any feelings at all that didn't revolve around yourself."

Daphne stormed off and Professor Kelly slammed the door shut.

"Was that a weird interview? Or is it just me?" Sheffley asked.

Gina laughed. "Trust me, Sheffley. This is *not* the weirdest it can get with Daphne at an interview. Not even close."

5.

"The DJ boyfriend was credible. Didn't know about Professor Kelly and tried for multiple days to get in touch with Amber before calling her parents." Miguel shook his head. "He truly didn't seem to know what had happened to her."

"Yeah, the professor didn't seem to know about the DJ either," Sheffley answered.

"Not surprising." Gina took a sip of her soda. They were back at the conference room with the papers everywhere on the table. "I'm sure she went to great lengths to keep each relationship from the other."

"So, we're back to square one." Miguel picked up a piece of paper just to let it fall dramatically back to the table. Instead, it floated gently and landed a foot from where he intended it to, sailing through the air like a leaf on a breeze. "No one knew anyone who'd want to hurt her."

"What if it's not a man?" Daphne asked. When all eyes turned to her, she started chewing her chips loudly.

"Are you sensing something?" Sheffley asked.

"Has Amber's spirit reached out?" Miguel was a millisecond behind Sheffley.

Daphne chewed and stared for what felt like forever. People hated uncomfortable silences, but Daphne loved them. The truth lived in moments of silence. Clarity stepped forward in the seconds of stillness. People were always clouding those moments with blabbering words that said nothing at all.

The silence said so much more.

But it was Gina who finally broke it. "Professor Kelly did say he had affairs with other students. There could be lots of jealous women in his wake."

Miguel had to comment. "This guy sounds like a real piece of work."

"He was quite the ladies' man back in the day apparently," Sheffley said in a tone that was almost reverent.

"We're not commending his predatory behavior of impressionable college students." Gina wagged a finger to scold Sheffley like an old school marm.

"No." Daphne announced her answer soundly, switching the conversation back to what she was sensing.

The rest of the team waited a beat for her to elaborate what she was denying with her firm answer, but when no explanation came Miguel had to ask, "No, you aren't sensing anything? Or what?"

"Exactly." Daphne chomped on another chip. "I'm just throwing out ideas same as all of you. Some part of her must've cared about both those men. But we can't be so biased as to assume the attacker was male. Especially if she was lured by someone she knew. Or poisoned. Or attacked from behind with chloroform."

"Now you're just grasping at straws." Sheffley waved a hand at Daphne as if to dismiss her contributions thus far.

"And you're not?" Daphne asked with a hard edge to her tone.

"Is there any way to reach out to her spirit, Daph?" Miguel asked. "Maybe we just ask her."

Daphne snorted. "It's not like I can just call her on a cell phone. Other than holding a séance—which is incredibly unreliable—there is no way to summon the spirit you want to talk to. You have to find them. I'm in the same boat as all of you."

"Okay. So we need to find the body," Gina tossed out to the group. "Has anyone scanned the database for Jane Does recovered over the past forty years? Unless the perp is the world's best body dumper, she was likely found by now."

"Or she's alive." Daphne raised an eyebrow. When everyone turned again, holding their breath assuming she had answers they didn't, she had to add with a shrug, "What? I'm just tossing out ideas."

Ignoring Daphne, Miguel turned back to Gina.

"Good idea. Can you chase that down? I want to interview the roommate. I find it weird that she didn't think anything of Amber not coming home for three days."

"Oh, yes," Daphne shouted, snapping her fingers at Miguel. "And see what she knows about the necklace."

"She what?" Miguel was honestly shocked at this outburst. It seemed like the most useful thing Daphne had said thus far during the conversation.

"Hmmm." Daphne had to ask herself where this information was coming from. It was such a natural revelation she hadn't stopped to think if maybe all along she *was* sensing something. "I don't know. I just have this feeling like the necklace is important and the roommate knows something."

Crunch. She popped another chip in her mouth and chewed loudly.

"I don't remember seeing anything about a necklace in any of the reports, Miguel." Gina stood and began ruffling through the pages as if the answer would magically appear and all truths would be revealed.

"There wasn't anything," Miguel answered. "No one reported it as missing when Amber disappeared. I'm guessing it felt inconsequential compared to a missing person. But Mike Benton mentioned it to me when I talked to him. A gift from her grandmother and she always wore it, but the roommate told him Amber was *not* wearing it to work that day for some reason. And yet it's never turned up." Miguel looked back at Daphne. "But you think the roommate has it?"

Daphne closed her eyes. "An oval shaped pendant made of tiny diamonds? Wow. It's beautiful." She opened her eyes and asked Miguel, "Is that it?"

"We'd have to ask someone. I don't know. But I do know it was diamonds and very valuable."

"Yep. The roommate doesn't have it. But I think...?" Daphne trailed off, looking at the ceiling.

"Yes? What is it you're sensing, Daphne?"

"I think the roommate knows a lot more than she

let on." Daphne smiled smugly and cocked her head to one side, her wild blonde hair shifting like stalks of corn in a breeze. "Told you. Cudda been a woman."

Miguel laughed in spite of the fact he was also excited at the first new piece of information in this case for forty years. "All right. I'll work on finding Maggie the roommate and Gina will chase down any possible Jane Does that we can link to our vic."

"I'll chase down locations of any other friends and family from the police report so we can find them easily if we need to interview them," Sheffley added.

"And I'm tired of doing all the heavy lifting here." Daphne popped another chip in her mouth and smacked as she chewed. "So I'll just sit here and look pretty."

6.

"Do you really think the necklace is the lynchpin here?" Miguel asked Daphne as he grabbed her hand and pulled her next to him on the couch. They were inside Daphne's tiny apartment, spending what little time they had these days alone with each other.

And Miguel couldn't help it. He had spent too many years in law enforcement to have Daphne leave his house after the sun went down. She either stayed all night or they hung out at her place. Yes, he logically knew Daphne could handle herself. He was constantly reminding himself of things he'd seen her do firsthand. But it didn't matter. There was always still a giant knot in his stomach thinking about her safety and all the vile things that *could* happen.

Too many years as a homicide detective to just

turn all that off.

"No, I don't," Daphne stated flatly. "I think the story is full of young adult assholes that this poor girl was surrounded by. But that doesn't make them kidnappers or murderers." She rested her head on Miguel's shoulder, still holding his hand. "We need to find her. It's as simple as that."

Miguel took both arms and wrapped them around Daphne, pulling her close. Now that his shoulder was fully healed from the gunshot wound chasing the Born Stars, he enjoyed being able to hug Daphne.

"Remember back when I thought you were crazy?" Miguel smiled as he spoke. Daphne couldn't see it with her eyes, but she saw it in her mind. Like Daphne herself, Miguel didn't smile very often, so it lit up the room when he did. She didn't even mind that it was at her expense. If she had doubts about anything in this world, it wasn't about how he felt about her.

"As if you don't now." Daphne rolled her eyes at no one in particular.

"I know you're not crazy. I think you're gifted." He kissed the top of her head to accentuate his words.

"Duncan once told me that he and I were a lot alike. Did I ever tell you that?" Daphne shifted so she could look Miguel in the eye. When Miguel simply shook his head, she continued. "He never elaborated, but I think he meant because we both had lonely childhoods and we spend our adulthoods making up for it by talking to ghosts."

"To help the living," Miguel added as a reminder to Daphne. She had a tendency to focus on all that she did for people who had died, but she did so much more for the people left behind, and he didn't want to lose sight of that.

Daphne half-smiled. "To help the living." She folded her arms and leaned into the couch, still turned to face Miguel. "Why are we obsessed with death, though? We both could do many things with our gifts. Why this?"

"You have a clarity that most people don't have when it comes to death." Miguel couldn't help it—he grabbed Daphne's hand and held on to it tightly this time. "Most of us are confused about our mortality, at best. And that's if we think about it at all. Thinking about it all being over and what happens next?" Miguel shook his head. "That's scary. And then you lose someone...you have to start thinking about it. And you want to believe but those doubts you've carried around forever still nag at you from the back of your mind." He locked eyes with Daphne. "You remove those doubts, Daphne. And not many people can. Even priests and pastors can't give the assurances you can."

"Talented doesn't mean I'm not crazy." Daphne made sure to remind him she was aware of her unique personality traits.

"So, you're a non-conformist. I think it's what makes you beautiful."

"Beautiful?" The skepticism was written all over Daphne's face. She'd been called many things, but never beautiful. "That's Alanna Savage. Not me."

Daphne's reaction gave Miguel a good laugh.

"You look just like your mother."

Daphne stood up and backed away, as if the accusation of her beauty were some disgusting morsel of rotten, smelly beef. Her lip curled up in disgust. "I don't think so. I am far from the beauty queen my parents wanted me to be."

"Why would your parents worry about your scarring from Stryker if they believed you had no chance at being a star of the silver screen?" At the horror plastered on Daphne's face, Miguel quickly pivoted his line of logic. "It's not a bad thing, Daphne. You cut your hair short because your mother hates it and style it like you stuck your finger in a light socket, but it hides nothing. You're beautiful. Inside and out."

"Well, there's where you're wrong." Daphne crossed her arms and pouted. "I don't style my hair at all."

"Face it, Daph." Miguel stood up and pulled Daphne close. "You could have been a movie star."

Daphne stuck her fingers in her ears and sang an

unmelodious rendition of la-la-la's.

Miguel pulled her fingers out of her ears and shouted to overcome the tuneless singing. "There are a small handful of us who appreciate you just as you are." He kissed her cheek near her ear and the singing stopped. "And I'm glad you chose to help ghosts and not be a movie star." He pulled out her hand and kissed the top of it. "Because then I'd have to share you with your adoring fans."

"First of all, there would never be any fans. People like me don't have those." Daphne placed her free hand on her hip, but she didn't pull the other away from Miguel. "Secondly, I hate film sets."

Miguel nodded and then pulled her close, breathing in deeply. Her wild hair smelled like a rainstorm. "I can imagine. They probably remind you of your absentee parents."

Daphne snorted. "That doesn't help by any means, but no. Movie sets are riddled with dark spirits." Miguel pulled his head back and stared at Daphne with a puzzled look. "There's a lot more dark arts going on around there than you could possibly know."

"You're wrong by the way." Miguel held her close again.

"I'm not. Lots of deals you don't want the details on."

"No." Miguel kissed her neck and she didn't pull away. "I meant about your adoring fans. You already have a bunch of those."

"Ha!" At this, Daphne pulled away, flapping her arms flamboyantly as she paced around her living room. "Name three."

"I can name a lot more than three." Miguel used his fingers to dramatically point out all the people who cared about her. "Gina. Sheffley. Duncan. My mother. My father." Daphne groaned loudly. "Ethan Bender's family. Madison Laurens' family. Grace Collins' family."

"You're stretching things here." Daphne still flapped in protest.

"Winston Cayman. His son, Derek."

"You've listed a bunch of people who appreciate my talents. *That's* what they're fans of. Not me. Very few people can tolerate the real me." Daphne folded her arms across her chest again and leaned on one hip.

Miguel walked to her with a smirk still dancing on his lips. He smoothed one of her chunks of hair that had taken on a mind of its own. Miguel was always smoothing her rougher edges. "You're right. Who could tolerate someone who's brave?" He kissed her cheek again. "Or someone compassionate?" He kissed her other cheek. "And bold?" Her forehead. "And in tune with the world." Her nose. "And beautiful." He kissed her lips and she didn't argue or pull away. She didn't necessarily agree with him, but she knew he believed it and it warmed her heart to have someone who loved her so unconditionally.

It was all she'd ever wanted when she was growing up in a lonely mansion. She'd daydreamed so many times of a family member or friend who knew what she could do and loved her anyway.

Maybe Cayman had been right. Maybe she *had* been destined to end up with a cop.

But the feelings of acceptance were a strange double-sided sword. They scared her as much as comforted her. So, she did what she always did when things got too close and comfortable.

She changed the subject. "I have a message for your mother from your grandmother." Miguel was still so close she could smell him and feel his warm breath as it mixed with her own. The day-old stubble on his chin prickled her own.

"Is that so?" He held her tightly. And he didn't pull away. His lips were millimeters from hers. She could only nod in response. "Well, you can tell Abuelita to come back later." He kissed her again and then scooped her up like a babydoll.

Some part of her brain was screaming at her to protest, but she had no idea why. Her heart felt secure here being held by this man.

"Let's get married." Miguel blurted. He wasn't

smiling and he didn't appear to be kidding. In fact, his face was as serious as Daphne had ever seen it. He had the same determination that he showed when he was about to arrest someone.

Daphne shrugged. "Okay."

Was she frightened of having love only to lose it? Hell, yes. Was she uncomfortable when someone was able to reach through her walls and hold her hand? Most definitely.

And Miguel was both of those things. She should be telling him no way. She should be jumping from his arms and barricading herself inside her bedroom.

Miguel was apparently just as surprised as she was at her response. "Really?"

Daphne squeezed her arms around his neck even as she rolled her eyes dramatically. "Why not? It's just the government's way of keeping tabs on what our souls already know is true."

Miguel smiled and rested his forehead against hers. "Spoken like a hopeless romantic."

She put a hand on his chest. "But no big wedding with a fancy party."

Miguel shook his head. "No way can I agree to that. My mom is going to want a big party."

Daphne frowned. "Then we just won't invite my family."

"Bullshit. I'm not marrying you without your family there."

"Fine. I'll invite Grandma Jean."

"No, Daphne. Your *alive* family there."

She paused, thinking about it. "I'm not wearing a white dress."

"I would die of shock if you did."

Daphne smiled. *Marriage*. It wasn't that she did or didn't want to marry Miguel. She hadn't lied when she said their souls were already one. She had just never imagined a world where anyone would want to marry her. And Miguel actually did. This handsome man with the perfect hair and a great career actually was choosing her.

"The necklace is a red herring, I think. We should find it, but I don't think it means as much as we want it to."

Miguel knew this tactic of hers as well as he knew he'd iron his jeans in the morning. And he took it as a good sign that she was actually happy but couldn't say those words out loud. He kissed her again in response.

"What did my grandmother want my mom to know?" Miguel asked as he carried Daphne toward her bedroom.

Daphne slouched a little and her cheeks turned red. "Not to serve pozole at the wedding. She wants tamales. And a mariachi band."

"So you knew this whole time? When I didn't even know?" Miguel laughed again.

This time, Daphne initiated the kiss. "It still meant everything when it came from you."

7.

A small sliver of light crept through the blinds in Daphne's bedroom, casting long shadows in dark corners. Beside her, Miguel sucked in deep breaths, sleeping soundly, not stirring at all.

But *something* had awakened Daphne.

She remembered ghosts visiting her at night before she even attended elementary school. She must have been a beacon for them because they would wake her up and beg her to give their loved ones a message. In those days, it mostly just annoyed her that they would interrupt her sleep for a fool's errand. What would a four-year-old do with such a message?

But as an adult, she was on high alert for spirits that needed her. Because now she was able to find those loved ones and share the message from beyond the grave.

"Daphne."

Her eyes followed the sound of the whispered voice, but nothing but shadows appeared. Daphne climbed out of bed, careful not to wake Miguel. She knew he slept with his handgun in the drawer next to his bed, and part of her worried needlessly that he may get scared by a ghost one night and shoot without thinking.

"I'm here," Daphne whispered back into the darkness. "What can I do?"

"Find me."

She spun to face the voice that whispered behind her ear. Nothing but darkness met her eyes. "Where are you?"

Silence and shadows. Daphne searched in the darkness, using all her senses. Someone was here with her. She knew it. She spun her head quickly to the left and then the right, searching for the entity she knew was there and wanting to confirm with her eyes what her senses knew to be true.

"Daphne. Please." Daphne heard the weeping first before she saw the figure. A young woman with brown curly hair sat on the foot of Daphne's bed inches from where Miguel lay sleeping. Her neon sweatshirt hung off one shoulder and she buried her face in her hands crying softly.

Daphne couldn't help but gasp as the realization hit her.

This was Melissa Amber Daniels. "I can help you, Amber. But you need to tell me who did this. And where I can find you."

Daphne was careful to keep whispering, but the volume was growing louder as the adrenaline filled her. This was the break they'd been needing.

Amber's ghost shook her head, her face still covered by her hands. The weeping continued. "I'm so alone. I just don't want to be alone anymore."

Daphne moved closer to the missing girl's spirit. She had long suspected that Amber hadn't made it, but until she saw the ghost with her own eyes a tiny part of her had held out hope. Now she knew Amber was indeed another soul in need of justice. Which was Daphne's specialty anyway. "You're not alone anymore, Amber. Stay with me. Lead me to your body."

"He told me he loved me." Amber wept.

Daphne had to choke back her own tears, such was the complete sadness that was overtaking her from Amber's emotions. More than sadness. Emptiness. Despair. Daphne physically shook her arms to loosen the grip of hopelessness that was emanating from the ghost in her bedroom.

"Who, Amber? Who hurt you?" Daphne knelt before the weeping ghost.

"He loved me." Amber finally let her hands drop and she lifted her face toward Daphne. "And he did this to me."

Daphne recoiled and covered her mouth to prevent too much sound from escaping. Ghosts appeared to her in a gamut of stages. The freshly dead often did appear very similarly to the way they'd died.

This was a forty-year-old murder, and yet Amber was still presenting her wounds from death.

And it was horrific.

Someone had smashed her face in. The flesh was barely hanging on to the broken cheek bones, her nose completely gone. One eye was simply not there, completely devoid of a socket in which to contain it. Someone had beaten her with anger and hatred. Daphne stepped back again as if the beatings would somehow transfer on to her.

And then she felt the frozen ground crunch beneath her feet. Daphne was outside and the evening air was brisk. She shivered and rubbed her arms from the night chill that washed over her as she stood in only Miguel's oversized T-shirt.

She saw Amber's car parked near a tree line. She began running toward it when she heard the unmistakable thud. It was January, so the trees offered no disguise to the violent event taking place on the other side of the car.

As she rounded the front of the car, she could barely make out a man's back with his arm high in the air. The passenger door was open and it obscured much of the view. But Daphne knew well enough what she was witnessing. The arm in the air held something long and metal. A pipe, maybe? And then it slammed down with tremendous force.

Daphne found it strange that the woman receiving these blows was alert enough to let out the ear-shattering scream.

But then she realized that the scream came from her own mouth, and she sat up in her own bed, dripping sweat despite the fact that she had been standing in freezing temperatures just an instant ago.

"Daphne?" Miguel shot up in bed, instantly alert, the panic in his voice matching her own. He looked around trying to determine where the threat came from.

And then it all came crashing down around her. Amber's sadness. The murder scene. The complete and utter violence. Daphne dropped her face into Miguel's shoulder and began to cry.

His heart still pounded vibrantly as he processed the scene, but deciding Daphne's tears were now the most momentous thing in the bedroom, he wrapped his arms around her and held her tight. Seeing her cry was one of the most frightening things he'd ever encountered, and he wasn't exactly sure what it meant. He rubbed her back soothingly as he continued looking around the room, searching for the culprit, even as he knew there was a high likelihood it was nothing he could see anyway.

"I saw her die," Daphne sobbed into Miguel's shoulder. "I saw it. I saw him kill her."

That got his attention. He pulled her back to look at her tear-stained face. "Who? Amber? You saw Amber die?"

"Yes. It was horrible." Daphne took a deep breath, trying to stop the emotions that were overtaking her. This was one of her least favorite things about her abilities. "Someone beat her to a pulp."

"Oh, Daphne." He wiped the tears from her face with a gentleness Daphne hadn't expected. "That's so awful."

"She was crying, and now I'm crying. Because he said he loved her."

"What a terrible thing to witness, Daphne. I'm so sorry." Miguel pulled her in close. She hugged him back because it felt warm and secure. She needed to feel his presence and convince herself she was no longer standing by trees watching a murder take place.

"I'm okay. I'm okay, Miguel." She pulled away enough to wipe the tears from her eyes but remained close enough to still feel his shirtless skin. "Sometimes their emotions overpower me."

Miguel shook his head. "I'm so glad I stayed tonight. I don't like the idea of you waking up to something like that and being all alone."

The sudden change in Daphne's tone occurred with an energy Miguel could feel as much as see. The air stilled and hovered around them like a balloon about to burst. Daphne stared hard at Miguel, looking deep within his eyes.

He knew she was ready for business. This was the Daphne he was familiar with. The woman on a mission to save all beings, alive or dead.

"I saw the necklace, Miguel."

"Amber's grandmother's gift? The diamond pendant?" Miguel asked, needing confirmation even though he felt confident that he knew the answer.

Daphne nodded. "She was wearing it. Amber *did* leave for work that night with the necklace on."

Miguel swore under his breath. "So the roommate was lying."

Daphne nodded again, her nostrils flaring from the anger and other emotions building up inside her. The energy had to go somewhere, so Daphne stood up, the sweat from her murderous vision still causing her T-shirt to cling to her body. A man had murdered a young woman in the prime of her life. And someone else had lied about it.

"I saw it, Miguel. I saw him beat her face in with a pipe or something long and metal." Daphne began pacing, arms flailing. Lose the energy, escape the emotions.

Miguel simply nodded, knowing he was powerless to stop the process Daphne was going through. "Can you identify the killer?"

Daphne twisted her hands this way and that. "I only saw his back, but…" She froze and looked directly at Miguel.

At her sudden pause, the energy in the room transferred to Miguel and he shot out of bed. "What? What is it?"

"I saw the crime scene." Daphne and Miguel locked eyes as the reality of Melissa Amber Daniels' fate began to get a little bit clearer. "I think I know where he killed her."

8.

"Is this what you saw in your vision?" Miguel asked Daphne, standing in the middle of a parking lot and staring at the trees in front of them. The morning sun was low in the sky but already warming the earth.

Daphne closed her eyes to lock in the memory of what she'd seen last night. Of course, at that time she'd been focused on the event happening on the other side of Amber's car, but there was no mistaking the tree line.

Opening her eyes to the present, Daphne pointed across the lot. "That's where her car was parked, but parallel to the curb. Not in a parking space."

"I believe you." Miguel turned Daphne to face him, and he rubbed her arms. "Before I call this in, do you know if he buried her here? Because he didn't leave the car here."

Daphne walked slowly across the parking lot, toward the scene she'd witnessed last night. The horror of the event still gave her chills, twisting her stomach at the memory of such violence.

Off to her right, a family sat on a picnic blanket eating snacks and enjoying the day. Daphne rolled her eyes at their ignorance. If they only knew what happened just a few feet from where they cavorted, they wouldn't be smiling and laughing right now.

Daphne stopped at the tree line, holding her hands up to feel the truth. "Amber. Where are you?"

Miguel walked up behind Daphne and wisely remained quiet. How he so intuitively knew when to be there and what to do, Daphne could only suppose. It was just one of those things people could sense without needing psychic abilities.

The leaves were soft beneath her feet, a stark contrast to the dried, frozen crunch of her vision. But this was the right spot. Amber was here somewhere.

"Daphne."

Daphne scanned the tree line. She knew that voice. "Amber?"

Miguel copied Daphne and looked all around for the ghost of their missing victim. He saw nothing, but he knew when Daphne saw her by the sudden change in her body.

Daphne froze and stared at the air in front of her. Miguel froze, too, watching Daphne closely.

"Amber. We need to find your body. Is this where he dumped you?"

Miguel waited patiently for the answers only Daphne could hear.

Amber, still battered and wearing a neon sweatshirt, pointed at the ground beneath her feet and then began to cry into her hands again.

Daphne turned to Miguel to interpret. "She's here. He dumped her body in this area." Daphne gestured with her hand to the general area where Amber was standing and weeping amongst the trees.

"I'm calling it in." Miguel walked back toward the

parking lot to make his calls. The picnickers must've heard or sensed something, because Daphne watched as the mother scurried to pack up her children and the picnic and walk rapidly toward their minivan.

Nothing like a forty-year-old crime scene and a bizarre psychic medium to ruin a good day.

But still, Daphne smiled as she watched them leave in a panic. Here was a mother who instinctively knew she needed to protect her family, without having any context to the actual events. She would know later when she saw it on the nightly news, but for now she only thought of putting her children first. Shielding their innocence. Keeping them safe from unseen horrors.

It was the kind of mother she wished Alanna had been. It was the kind of mother she hoped she'd be one day.

And then she jolted in shock at her own thoughts.

She had never, *never*, wanted children. This was a dark, dark world where people were cruel. They left you alone to fend for yourself. You never knew who you could trust. And then you die. She had never wanted to bring an innocent human into this world and let them be subjected to its horrors and betrayals.

But then she looked up at Miguel on his phone and the moment they made eye contact, he winked at her with a half-smile. An image of Duncan popped into her head. Two men who had believed in her when no one else had. They would never leave her alone or betray her.

She shrugged off the warm feeling. Could this be what it felt like to know hope? It was hard to balance her natural cynicism with such a feeling of optimism. She wasn't even sure she liked feeling hopeful. It was vulnerable in a way she hated to be.

So instead of dwelling on it, she turned to the matter at hand.

"You don't have to keep looking like a scene from a horror movie, Amber." Her voice was more biting than she meant it to be.

The ghost's face shot up from her hands, her

empty eye socket a bullseye from which Daphne could barely look away.

"He did this to me. I don't want anyone to forget."

This softened Daphne a little. Retribution. Now that was a feeling she could rally behind. "We won't, Amber. We never could. And we're going to catch him. Do you remember his name, by chance?"

"They're on their way and so is Gina." Miguel stomped up behind her and Amber disappeared.

"Miguel!" Daphne whined. He held up his hands to ask what and she rolled her eyes. "You scared Amber away."

He shrugged. "Sorry?"

Daphne just groaned and stormed over to the tree line. How could she voice that she was just as mad at herself for dreaming of nonexistent children as she was at him for unwittingly scaring away their victim's spirit?

Miguel shook his head as he pulled out a pair of rubber gloves from his pocket. He could worry about

Daphne's dramatic state later. Right now he didn't want to lose the site that Daphne had indicated. He walked back to his trunk and grabbed two small flags that he then proceeded to place in the ground where Daphne had said.

"Is this right, Daph?" he asked over his shoulder, still down on his haunches.

Without turning around, Daphne called back, "Yes."

He walked back over to the tree line where Daphne leaned against an old oak with a large trunk. "Hey come on. We can interview the ghost later. If we find her body, that is a huge discovery. The family will finally have the opportunity to mourn her."

"We will."

"Will what?" Miguel raised an eyebrow.

"Find her body. That's where he buried her. Not even that deep. I'm surprised a dog hasn't accidentally stumbled across her remains after all these years. He beat her to death in a total rage and then dumped her right there, moved her car and left town." The final words came so naturally out of her mouth she hadn't processed them before she spoke them. But the information was new.

Daphne and Miguel locked eyes. *He left town.*

"So, she had a *third* boyfriend?" Miguel asked wide-eyed. He hadn't been a loner like Daphne, but he was hardly Mr. Popularity in high school and college. Even dating one girl at a time had always been challenging. But to balance three? That took some energy. "How did she keep them all from one another?"

Daphne swallowed hard and then looked at the tiny flags sticking out of the dirt. Solitary little reminders, almost insignificant, that a once vivacious young woman had once had her whole life before her and it was extinguished in a flash. "Apparently, she didn't."

"So, a jealous rage? But it had to be somewhat premeditated. They were in *her* car and he had a lead pipe with him?" Miguel shook his head. "It doesn't make sense."

"Both things can be true." And then Daphne remembered that Miguel couldn't quite read her mind. "Premeditation and a jealous rage." She walked back to where the flags commemorated Amber's death, hands outstretched with palms facing down.

She wanted answers that only the dead could now provide.

"Miguel. Daphne." Gina slammed her car door shut and jogged to where they stood just inside the trees. "You saw Amber?"

Daphne frowned as she nodded. There was that feeling again: hope. It was lighting up Gina's face like a spotlight.

"She visited Daphne last night and showed her a vision. This guy told Amber he loved her, apparently, and then beat her face in with a lead pipe and dumped her over where Daphne's standing." In this way Miguel caught Gina up to speed with what Daphne had uncovered so emotionally in the past twelve hours.

"So, it was one of the boyfriends, huh?" Gina

asked Daphne, who simply stared in return. This interrogation was really dampening her ability to get clues from the scene.

So Miguel answered, "Yeah, but not the two you're thinking. We think there may have been a third boyfriend who skipped town after the murder."

"So, her extracurricular activities finally caught up to her," Gina muttered. The sound of the forensics van pulling up forced her to turn and look behind her.

"Yeah, we're thinking jealousy," Miguel explained.

Gina whipped her head back around. "But what about the damned necklace? Something doesn't fit."

Miguel shook his head. "Maybe that was just a crime of convenience. The roommate wanted it. Took it when she was out of the picture."

Gina looked at Daphne who remained stoic. "Maybe," she said, but she said it in a way that told Miguel she didn't really buy it.

"What do we have here?" Victoria De La Torre

from the Coroner's office sauntered up to Daphne and Miguel. She was dressed in a beige pantsuit, her hair brushed and long down her back.

"Victoria. Hi. Forty-year-old homicide," Miguel explained. "We have reason to believe the remains of our vic are between those two flags. Where Daphne is standing." He pointed and Daphne waved.

Victoria smiled at the blonde psychic. "Daphne Winters? I've heard so much about you. It's a pleasure to meet any woman who has the entire Fresno Police Department hanging on her every word."

Daphne stomped over to the Medical Examiner and stuck out her hand. "And it's a pleasure to meet a woman who has a like-minded desire and ability to get answers from the dead."

Victoria laughed as she shook Daphne's hand. "Yes. I find there is a very small cabal of people who actually listen to the dead." Victoria leaned in conspiratorially and whispered in Daphne's ear, "I'd love for you to do a reading for me some time."

Daphne pulled back and wrinkled her nose. "There are as many ghosts following you around as there are me."

Victoria laughed again. "I really like you." And then Victoria became serious as a C.E.O. as she began instructing her team. "Tommy, I want photographs before and after we dig. Everything documented." Tommy, a young man with a fancy, high-end camera, nodded in affirmation to the instructions.

As Victoria stepped forward to join her team at the site of the burial, Daphne grabbed her arm. "But you carry a dark secret. Your own mother. You got into this line of work because of your mother's murder. She was shot in bed while she slept. And you were five." Daphne dropped her hand as she realized how awful this memory must be for Victoria. "And there in the house."

Victoria smiled sadly, but she wasn't shocked that Daphne had outed her secret. "We all have our reasons for talking to the dead." She looked at Miguel and Gina as if daring them to argue. "My mother is mine."

"Your mother is proud of you. Very proud," Daphne stated.

Victoria wiped a tiny tear just as it began to form. "Is she here?"

Daphne nodded. "She's always with you."

Miguel cleared his throat. He knew Daphne's reputation for exposing family secrets, but he had never before been a firsthand witness. He suddenly felt awkward and nervous knowing something about Victoria De La Torre that he wasn't supposed to know. "Sorry for your loss."

Unable to make eye contact with the M.E. he worked so closely with, he stared at his foot as he rubbed a place in the dirt near the tree line.

Victoria placed a gentle hand on Miguel's arm. "I appreciate your kindness, Miguel, but I have healed from her death thirty years ago." She looked over at Daphne. "But the hole in my heart from missing her hasn't, so thank you, Daphne. I am relieved beyond words to know she is always with me."

Daphne knew people should smile in a moment like this, so she forced one side of her mouth in an upward direction. It looked more like she was pensive, but it was the best she could do. "She is. She watches over you. And she says to tell you she is perfectly fine. Her death was quick and she feels no pain or anger now."

Victoria smiled, a real smile, back at Daphne. "That's good to hear."

And then Daphne's eyebrows tightened with concern. "But there's a dark spirit following you too. He's angry. Your mother keeps him at bay, but he…*hates* you."

Unconcerned, Victoria continued smiling. "I bet he does."

"You know this dark spirit?" Gina asked, completely enthralled in the discovery of Victoria's drama.

Victoria nodded. "It's the man who murdered my mother."

"Good. I'm glad they caught him." Miguel puffed

out his chest as if he would be hunting him down himself if he hadn't been already caught.

"Not good." Daphne shook her head. "It's her father."

Victoria blew out a heavy breath. "You don't pull any punches, do you?"

Sensing she'd gone too far, Daphne frowned. "Still like me?"

Victoria surprised Daphne by pulling her into a hug. "Yeah, I do. I really, really do." She pulled back from a stunned Daphne. "I wish there were more people like you in this world. There are too many secrets."

Daphne could only offer one gift in return for Victoria's respect. "I'll keep an eye on him for you."

Victoria nodded, warmth filling her eyes. "I trust you." Sucking in a large breath of air and rolling back her shoulders, Victoria transformed back into her businesslike persona. "Now. To find your forty-year missing vic."

9.

"We just need the story on the necklace. I'm hoping this is fairly quick and painless," Miguel stated to Gina and Daphne as they pulled up to a nondescript apartment building in the middle of Fresno. These apartments were only a few miles from where the roommate had lived with Amber back in the eighties. It was almost as if time had frozen still for Margaret "Maggie" Hicks.

"Looks like Maggie didn't do much with her college degree." Gina wrinkled her nose at the judgment of the apartment building. "Didn't we get called to an investigation here once?"

They all climbed out of the car with very little gusto.

"Yeah. The Soto case." Miguel nodded to Gina as

they walked.

"There are a lot of random people living in apartments. Just because you had a murder here once doesn't mean anything about Maggie," Daphne stated. She wasn't entirely sure why they were judging, but she could sense that they were. And *she* lived in an apartment and had never murdered anyone.

"It's just…these apartments are *known* in the law enforcement community, Daphne. It's unusual for anyone to choose to live here if they had anywhere else to go," Miguel explained. "Apartment 21C." He pointed the ladies in the direction of Maggie's apartment. "And also Amber's boyfriend the DJ? He's living in a mansion. So it's quite an interesting situation."

"Different life goals." Daphne stated the facts as she knew them.

Gina laughed. "That's a nice way of putting it."

Miguel knocked on the door of apartment 21C and then stood back and waited for Maggie-the-roommate to answer.

And when she did, the woman who stood before them clearly had had a very hard life. Her face was weathered and worn far beyond her sixty years. Her hair was fried past anything a brushing could fix from years of too much hair dye or narcotics or some crazy mix of both. Her teeth were the color of tea, like she had actually tea-stained her mouth. "Yeah?" And her voice was raspy from years of cigarettes.

"Maggie Hicks?" Miguel pulled out his badge when she nodded. "Miguel Alvarez, Fresno P.D. Cold Case division. This is my partner, Gina Malone, and our psychic medium consultant, Daphne Winters."

"And? Whaddya want?" She leaned on her doorframe as if the entire act of standing here talking to these people was just too much for her body to bear.

"We wanted to ask you some questions about Melissa Amber Daniel. May we come in?"

At the name, her face softened. "Did you find her?"

Gina jumped in. "Not yet. But we're re-opening

the case and hoping you can help with that actually."

Wordlessly, Maggie shoved the door all the way open and began walking inside. "I knew one day this would all come popping back up."

Miguel and Gina followed Maggie, and Daphne hung back, letting them lead the way. Maggie flopped on the ugliest and most beat-up couch Miguel had ever seen. He decided he'd prefer to stand anyway. Just the mere thought of sitting on the couch made him itchy from the bugs he knew must live in it.

"I know it's been a while, Miss Hicks, but can you tell me what you remember?" Gina sat across from the former roommate, unafraid of the dirty old couch, and led the questioning. From years on the service, Gina suspected someone like Maggie might be more receptive to Gina than Miguel anyway.

Maggie rolled her eyes melodramatically. "As if I could ever forget."

"Can you take us through the day she went missing?" Gina prodded.

"She hung out with her bubble-butt boyfriend Mike and then went to work. Up until she went missing, there was nothing remarkable about that day. I was studying for a science test so I had been hunkered down at the kitchen table, watching her come and go throughout the day." Maggie leaned back against the raggedy couch. "And didn't think anything of it at the time."

"When she left, how was she dressed?" Gina asked.

"Hair pulled back, red shirt for work. Again, nothing remarkable."

Maggie started into a coughing fit that lasted a few minutes. The investigators waited for her to regain her ability to breathe.

"What about her diamond necklace from her grandmother? The one she always wore?" Gina asked when Maggie had regained her composure.

"She was always wearing that. I don't know if she even took it off for showers. Never saw her without it."

"We spoke with Mike Benton and he said that *you* had the necklace," Miguel said, jumping in, sensing that he was catching the former roommate in a lie. You had to act when someone's tale didn't line up or the moment could pass you by and the liar would have time to adjust their story accordingly.

But Maggie turned stone cold eyes to Miguel and said, "Mike Benton is a fucking liar, detective."

"So, you never had the necklace in your possession?" Gina followed up.

Maggie's face tightened up like something in the room stunk like three-day-old garbage. "Why in the hell would I have Amber's necklace? She always wore it and had it on when she left."

"Perhaps you just didn't notice? And found the necklace later?" Miguel suggested.

"Detective." Maggie leaned forward and spoke slowly, overly enunciating, so the apparently moronic detective in her living room could understand. "If she hadn't been wearing her necklace, that would have been something to remember because she *always* wore it. I'm telling you, it's wherever she is."

"Miss Hicks, what reason would Mike have to lie to us about the necklace?" Gina wondered.

"Well, for starters, because he probably has it because he probably killed her." Maggie shook her head as she spoke to emphasize her opinion of Amber's old boyfriend.

Daphne announced, "No, he didn't kill her."

Maggie looked over at the blonde psychic but said nothing to argue with her.

And Miguel jumped in to soften any potential conflict between the two opinions. "What makes you believe Mike is behind her disappearance?"

Maggie leaned back and folded her arms across her chest. It was obvious she'd waited years to rat this guy out. "When I woke up the following morning, I noticed Amber's bed was neatly made and she was nowhere to be found. This was weird on two fronts because she was a total slob and never up before noon unless she had class. I called Mike that morning and told him I was worried about Amber, and he told me she was fine."

Miguel looked at Gina. "Those were his words? She was fine?"

Maggie nodded. "Yeah, he told me I was making a big deal out of nothing."

Miguel stole a glance at Daphne. Either Mike was lying or Maggie was because their stories contradicted one another.

Daphne nodded. Maggie was telling the truth.

Miguel turned back to Maggie. "Mike told me *you* weren't ever worried about Amber, and that finally he and Amber's mother got worried and called the police."

Maggie snorted. "He was semi-cute in the rock band way of the eighties, but beyond that I have no idea what Amber ever saw in him. He was so full of shit and arrogant to boot. Why he was so conceited even though he was just a dumb local DJ I'll never know."

"So he never expressed concern to you about Amber? Ever once?"

Maggie shook her head.

"And you never told him you had the necklace?"

"Even if I did ever have the necklace, which I absolutely did NOT, I don't know what purpose there would be to tell Mike. I hated him from the start. I certainly wouldn't confide in him." Maggie looked like she might puke.

"Miss Hicks, were you aware that Amber had a relationship with a professor named Stephen Kelly?" Gina said, continuing the questioning.

Maggie's eyes widened with unparalleled shock. "Professor Kelly? No. No way. She always said she hated that guy."

"And if we told you that she had a romantic relationship with him that he confirmed?" Miguel added.

Maggie's lip curled. "I guess she was really attracted to self-centered men." The former roommate shook her head. "There's no accounting for taste."

Gina leaned forward. "Miss Hicks. What do you think happened to Amber?"

Maggie Hicks didn't answer right away. She stared off into a far-off distance where big hair was the style and shoulder pads reigned supreme and Amber Daniel was still alive. The lines of her weather-worn face were deep with edges that, like an old statue, simply couldn't handle the pressure of time gone by.

"I tried to find her for years. I became obsessed, to be honest. My grades slipped. I never graduated. Never trusted any of my own relationships." She gestured around her apartment. "So it's no wonder I ended up alone. I don't know what happened to Amber. I truly, *truly* wish I did. Her absence left a void in my life that has never been filled." Maggie opened a drawer in her coffee table, took out a cigarette and lit it, taking a long drag as if it was the only way she could face this conversation. "But I'll tell you what." She pointed her lit cigarette toward Gina as she spoke. "There is no way you can convince me that Mike Benton isn't related somehow. He knows what happened to her even if he didn't do it himself. She shudda dumped him long before she did."

This caught Miguel's attention. "So Amber had broken up with Mike before she went missing?"

"Oh, yeah. Like the dingleberry that he is, she couldn't shake him from clinging to her ass, but she had woken up to his bullshit weeks before and ended their relationship." Another puff on the cigarette. "I hate that guy. So much."

Miguel opened his mouth to ask another question, but the sound of his phone ringing interrupted his thoughts. He walked outside to take the call. And Gina took this moment to thank Maggie for her help, committed to keeping her in the loop of the investigation, and then she and Daphne followed Miguel out front, leaving the former roommate to close the door behind them as she finished the only thing that could comfort her from the ruin that Amber's disappearance had made of her life.

It wasn't just Amber's parents who suffered from the not knowing. Amber may be the one who was missing, but Maggie had also forever been changed that fateful January day. The collateral damage from a crime rippled out far beyond what anyone could anticipate. Just the happenstance from living with a woman who went missing had turned Maggie's life upside down and she'd ended up in a dead-end career and living on the wrong side of town.

Hanging up his phone, Miguel turned to Gina. "That was Victoria. They found what they can confirm are human remains. They'll need to check the DNA before identifying who they found but…"

"It's Amber," Daphne stated with absolute confidence. She didn't need DNA to know it.

"I think we knew where this was headed, but we're now investigating a homicide, not a missing persons case." Gina folded her arms as she considered all that they had recently uncovered. "So, what about Maggie's details? They sure don't paint the golden boy in a positive light."

Miguel looked at Daphne before answering. "Maybe their memories are just fuzzy after all these years?"

Daphne rolled her eyes. "You don't need to be psychic to see that Amber's disappearance affected this woman's life."

Gina laughed. "And that she hated DJ Bendy."

"Well, I definitely never pretended to be psychic," Miguel said. "I guess we go back and talk to Bendy again. This time with the confidence that she's been murdered and dumped in Roeding Park." He frowned. It never got any easier to have to announce that someone was murdered.

Gina nodded. "That should sober him up. Let's wait for confirmed identity and cause of death before heading over."

"We don't need to wait," Daphne announced.

"I know that and you know that," Gina responded to Daphne. "But Mike Benton doesn't know that. I want a report in hand and then we can see how he reacts."

"Is it a waste of time, Daph?" Miguel asked the blonde psychic. "You saw the killer and it was some new guy."

Daphne shrugged. "I don't know. Just because he didn't hold the murder weapon doesn't mean he wasn't involved somehow. You heard the roommate. And whatever else she may be, she's not a liar. At least, she wasn't lying to us."

"Sheffley and I will work on trying to uncover who else she might have been dating," Gina announced. "You two find out why the DJ lied after all these years. And Miguel?" Gina continued when Miguel made eye contact. "Ask Victoria about that necklace. Whatever else, I do believe that Amber was wearing it when she left her apartment that day. If it isn't on the body, then the killer may have it."

10.

"Do you mind if we swing by my parents' house on our way to interview Mike Benton? My mom called while I was talking to Victoria." Miguel opened the car door for Daphne and guided her into the car. "I'm not sure what she needs from me but I want to check in with her."

"It's not for you. It's for me. Let's go." Daphne scowled and closed the door with far more gusto than was necessary.

The frost that had taken over Daphne's mood made Miguel shudder when he climbed into the driver's seat. "Is everything okay?"

Daphne shifted abruptly in her seat and faced Miguel head on, missiles aimed at the unsuspecting detective. "Why did you tell your mom about the wedding? I wasn't ready to tell people."

Miguel reacted as if he'd been slapped. "I was happy. Why should this be a secret? My mom's excited. What has you so upset? What did my mom do?"

Daphne let out a frustrated yell. "It's not your mom that's the issue. You know that." Daphne turned and rolled her eyes. "It's *my* mom."

Miguel shook his head. If he were any more confused his head would be floating. "What about your mom? I don't get it. Talk to me straight, Daph."

Daphne's lips were tight. Saying the words looked like it hurt physically as much as emotionally. "Your mom was excited so she called my mom. And my mom came here. To Fresno."

"That's great." Miguel's smile ended immediately once Daphne gave him a look of pure hellfire. "Why is it not great? I'm sure your mom just wants to help with everything."

"That's exactly why this isn't great." Daphne flopped back in the seat. "Just drive to your mom's house. I'll have to have the talk with Alanna at some point about what the boundaries are. Might as well be now."

Miguel turned the engine over and pulled out onto Shaw, heading for his parents' house. "I think you're a little hard on your mom, Daphne."

"No." Daphne wagged a finger at Miguel. "No, you don't get to judge my relationship with my mother when yours is a sweet lady and mine is an overbearing narcissist."

"Okay. But what if you gave her the benefit of the doubt for once? Maybe she truly wants to build a relationship with her only daughter. Who's been estranged for ten years."

"Do I believe that deep, deep within the soul of the fluff and nonsense that is Alanna Savage that an actual human being with compassion for others actually exists?" Daphne made huge pretense of debating the ridiculous thought in her mind. "Maybe. But that's not what this is. She's here for herself. I can just sense it."

Miguel took his eyes off the road for one brief moment before reaching over and squeezing Daphne's hand. "You know I trust your intuition. But I do think it gets cloudy when your mother is involved."

Daphne snorted. "On the contrary. I haven't needed psychic abilities to read Alanna Savage since I was five years old." Daphne looked out the window, watching the houses get quainter and quainter as they zoomed by. The only thing she had ever felt when it came to her mother was completely alone. "No, there's an angle in here for sure. I just don't know exactly what it is."

"Do you want to just interview the DJ and then come back to my mom's later?" Miguel asked earnestly. He knew enough that Daphne's relationship with her mother was at the very least complicated. And he wasn't sure how he felt about the showdown that could occur on his mother's front lawn.

"Nah. I definitely want to talk to the DJ, but I have to handle this first." She gestured out the front window and then let her hand flop back with a hard plop in her lap. "Just take me to your parents' house."

Miguel smiled to himself as he drove. "I think you're worried because she is going to want you to wear a fluffy white dress and hold brightly colored flowers."

Daphne didn't argue. "She's going to ruin it all for sure."

"Were you planning to just never tell her?" Miguel had to ask.

Truth be told, telling her parents hadn't really even entered her mind. They were such a small part of her life since she left Malibu ten years ago. Duncan was her real family. "I was probably going to tell them. Just to invite them as guests, like they are." Daphne shifted to face Miguel. "My mom isn't exactly your typical mother of the bride."

Miguel laughed out loud. "And you're not exactly the stereotypical bride-to-be."

Daphne turned away. "You're going to eat your words, Detective Alvarez. You imagine that everyone's family is like your family. But you'll see. When we get there. You'll see."

This sobered Miguel up. Did he assume all families were like his? He rubbed his clean-shaven chin. No, he knew far too well how dysfunctional families could be. He'd been called out to too many homicides that took place all within the family. Even the Amber Daniel case. Most likely it was someone she was close to and perhaps had even loved who had beaten her in Roeding Park and buried her body in a shallow grave.

He knew about dysfunction. He knew far too much about dysfunction and how it often ended.

He turned soft eyes to Daphne, and she knew immediately what he was thinking.

"Okay. Maybe not murder, but my mom is just a lot." Daphne frowned. "She's going to make it all about her."

Miguel shrugged. "Then maybe we just let her. I know neither you nor I care that much about the pomp and circumstance of the wedding. It's more for our families anyway."

Daphne shook her head. "I guess I'm not that big of a person. She's overshadowed my whole life. The one day. The *one* day that's mine and she's going to suck that up too."

Miguel held up a finger. "Allegedly."

Daphne grabbed his finger and pushed it away. "Psychic, remember? It's just a matter of time."

The moment Miguel turned onto the street of his family home, he was instantly aware that there was something going on. His parents had lived for decades on a quiet little street with trees hanging over sidewalks and casting shadows into the street. It wasn't exactly the posh side of town, but it wasn't the ghetto either. His parents had a nice, moderate home on a nice, moderate street.

But today there was commotion like this moderate street had never seen before.

Vans were parked haphazardly as if they had barely enough time to turn the wheel and cut the engine. People were blocking sidewalks and filling up driveways and streets with cameras, boom mics, lighting equipment—things Miguel rarely had seen even at press conferences for homicides.

"What the…?" Miguel quickly scanned for a place to park and found the only spot left for blocks. And it was a hefty walk from the Alvarez home.

"It's almost like I told you so." Daphne's voice was smug but her face reflected the same nervousness that Miguel was struggling to hide.

"All this? Is because your mom is in Fresno?" Miguel fought the urge to laugh at the ridiculousness of it all.

Daphne imitated reading a headline on a billboard above her head. "Washed up film actress condescends to head to Central Valley to ruin daughter's wedding."

Miguel turned wide eyes to Daphne. Were they going to need a press agent just to get married? "They're not going to ask us questions, are they?"

Daphne shrugged. "Probably. Just respond 'no

comment'. Whatever you say, they'll take the worst of it and you'll be an internet meme by tomorrow morning."

"Can't wait." Miguel climbed out of the car and then rounded the vehicle to help Daphne. He held her arm as they walked down the sidewalk toward his parents' house. Yes, he loved to be close to her, but truth be told, he was a little frightened that he would be asked something about his famous future mother-in-law, who he knew nothing about. He hoped Daphne would be better at handling them since she'd grown up in Hollywood.

As they neared the white bungalow, the press ignored them. What did they know about two non-celebrities going for a walk in the middle of the day? The couple almost made it to the house unscathed.

But when Miguel and Daphne were one house away from the Alvarez home, Alanna Savage, the Hollywood movie star and Daphne's estranged mother, opened the front door and made a big production about seeing her daughter.

"Daphne!" Alanna screamed her name as if she had come back from the dead. And then she ran full speed toward the young couple, grabbing Daphne and pulling her into a bear hug before she could even find the wherewithal to resist.

And then the mass of people filling the quiet street engulfed the trio with camera flashes, people talking over one another with questions and every bit of equipment known to man thrust into their faces.

Alanna Savage, being the professional star, soaked it all in. She beamed at the attention and the questions.

"Yes, this is my daughter, Daphne." Alanna spoke with the confidence and grace of royalty. Miguel didn't have the slightest clue how she'd even heard a question in the melee of garbled words that had come flying at them. "She lives here in your beautiful little hamlet, and I'm here to put on a wedding gala fit for a princess."

Someone shoved a microphone into Miguel's face so forcefully he thought for a brief moment about assault charges. "Are you the groom? Will you be marrying Alanna Savage's daughter?"

Miguel stole a glance at Daphne. "No comment?"

And then the attention shifted from the tall, dark, well kempt detective to the wild-haired blonde at his side. "How do you feel to know your mother will be helping you with your wedding planning?"

Miguel watched as Daphne flipped up her middle finger, stated, "Fuck off," and then marched into the Alvarez home, leaving Miguel and Alanna standing there dumbstruck

The throngs of people who'd been shouting over each other just moments before fell silent.

So much for Daphne being the expert at handling the press.

11.

Miguel found Daphne in his parents' backyard.

"I wanted to smash something but didn't want to do that to your mom," Daphne explained without looking at Miguel. "So I came out here where I risked less destruction."

Miguel smiled. "Well, that's personal growth."

They sat in silence for a while. There were birds chirping in the distance that provided a soundtrack to the moment. The azalea bush was just beginning to think about blooming despite the colder air. But the sky was blue and the sun felt good on Daphne's face.

"This would have been my life. If I had followed the dream my parents had laid out for me." Daphne turned to Miguel. "Reporters, gossip columns, parties. That's what my mom thrives on." Daphne looked at her feet. "And I will just always be in her shadow."

Miguel put two strong arms around her and pulled her close. Her hair smelled like hair product. He loved that they both spent time on their hair in the morning but with completely different outcomes. "You're in no one's shadow."

Daphne glared at him. "The wedding is supposed to be *our* day. And now it will be all about Alanna Savage, movie star."

"What if there's a way for everyone to be happy?" Miguel asked.

Without him even voicing his thoughts Daphne answered. "Yeah. That might actually work."

He kissed her forehead. "Are we ready to go back in and talk to mothers?"

Daphne shrugged. "What more is there to say? We need to interview an old boyfriend of a long dead young woman." Daphne squinted. "Who's standing in your backyard."

"Amber? She's here?" Miguel spun around

looking for the evidence with his own unseeing eyes.

Daphne grabbed him and angled him toward the back corner of the fenced-in yard. "There." She walked toward the young woman's ghost only she could see. "You look better," Daphne told Amber. "More like yourself."

Where she had let her injuries be her defining characteristics the last time Daphne saw her, with this apparition she chose to reflect how she'd looked in life. Her hair was poofed in the eighties style. Her oversized shirt dangled off one shoulder and her large earrings popped out of her permed brown hair like tree ornaments.

She looked like an eighties pin-up girl. Daphne could see why she struggled to manage her buffet of boyfriends.

"You found me." Amber allowed her relief to be felt. "It felt like so long, I wasn't sure anyone ever would."

"Who killed you, Amber? Can you give me a

name?" Daphne asked.

Amber nodded. "Barrett Thomas. He drove trucks for a company called Dynamite Trucking."

"How did you meet him?" Daphne asked, noticing a lightness to Amber that hadn't been there before. The simple discovery of her body had changed her spirit so immensely.

"The way I met most of my dates. At the diner."

"The Denny's on Shaw?" Daphne asked.

As Amber nodded, Miguel asked, "What? What's going on?" But Daphne shushed him so she could focus on Amber.

Daphne continued the interview. "How long had you known him?"

"We'd dated about six months. He was handsome, tall. He was older. I think that was what I liked most about him." Amber winked at Daphne and she recoiled at the gesture. "I guess I had a thing for mature men."

"How much older are we talking? Dr. Kelly

older?" Daphne tried unsuccessfully to hide her disgust. She had often seen young girls with dreams of becoming a star throwing themselves at her middle-aged father, and she'd always felt like it was such a degrading thing to do. She couldn't help the judgment that seeped into her soul.

But Amber just laughed. "No, nothing like that. He was twenty-eight with a career, and he owned his own home." She sighed at the memory. "I thought he was going to take me away from here."

Daphne allowed Amber's memories to flood her mind. In them she saw a vibrant young girl who had always been popular at school. And her smile was a mask to the world. She was seeking an escape from an abusive father and an alcoholic mother. Not completely apples-to-apples with Daphne's own lonely life, but similar enough that she understood instantly why Amber was escaping.

It was the same reason she had. Running from misery toward a new life.

"So that's the whole reason you went to college? Just to find an escape?" Even as Daphne asked, she knew the answer.

"I was just looking for a husband to get me out of here. Barrett lived in Northern California, and I envisioned being a homemaker while he provided for me and our children." She sighed again. She was a hopeless romantic. "I was so close to the life I dreamed of."

"So, when your ex-boyfriend Mike Benton says you wanted to be a schoolteacher...?" Daphne asked.

Amber's shoulders slumped. "That's what *Mike* wanted. His vision of our life together was vastly different than mine." She shrugged as if to say, 'what does it matter now.' "Once I knew Barrett was the one, I ended all my other relationships. Even Mike. Although he struggled to get it through his thick skull and even thicker ego."

Daphne translated over her shoulder for Miguel. "The roommate was right. She had ended things with Mike." Miguel stepped forward to ask follow-up questions and Daphne held up her hand to stop him. She turned back to Amber. "So if everything was so perfect with Barrett, why on earth did he kill you?"

Amber shook her head. "I had no idea he had such jealousy issues. I guess in hindsight I really didn't know him at all. He came through town once a month. Was I supposed to stay chaste sitting around and waiting for him when we hadn't committed to each other yet?"

Daphne nodded. "I had sensed the jealous rage."

"I also had no idea how he had found out about anything. I mean, again. He came through town once a month while he was driving through. He had no friends here or anything." She lowered her voice conspiratorially, more for show than anything since no one but Daphne could see or hear her. "Someone told him."

A flash of the diamond necklace Amber always wore popped into Daphne's mind, and she instantly knew that was the connection. "Whoever has the necklace is the one who ratted you out..."

"I hope you are pleased with yourself!" A furious Alanna Savage came storming out the back door of the Alvarez home. "You've gone viral in less than half an hour."

Daphne looked at Miguel. "Am I supposed to know what that means?"

Miguel smiled. "It means your gesture to the press is all over the internet."

Daphne rolled her eyes. "Mom. I am in the middle of something very important. I am talking to the ghost of the woman who was murdered forty years ago, and no one has ever been held accountable. Your stupid little internet problem is not important."

But when she looked back at the place where Amber's ghost had been a moment ago, she saw only flowers and bushes. Daphne groaned.

Alanna flopped her arms wildly and equally annoyed. "Ghosts. Always ghosts at a time like this. It's everywhere, Daphne. And not in a good way."

"That's not important. This is!" Daphne shouted

back.

Miguel felt out of his depth in the warring family, but he was a peace officer so he knew he couldn't just let this escalate here in the backyard. He stepped between them. "Ladies, please. You both have valid concerns. We can talk about them calmly and rationally."

Daphne folded her arms across her chest, but she did calm down. "I'd love to hear how you think her nonsense is valid."

"Her reputation is tied closely to her career. She had every reason to want to protect it," Miguel explained.

"You can't just alienate the press, Daphne. You can't recover from that," Alanna shouted over Miguel.

Miguel turned to his future mother-in-law, the stunning and glamorous Hollywood star. "And Daphne has made it her life's mission to solve crimes originally deemed unsolvable. She doesn't live in a world with press and reputations. And that's by design."

Alanna fought back tears, which only made

Daphne roll her eyes. With the most over-the-top flamboyance, Alanna asked, "So what do we do now?"

"I think we need some ground rules," Miguel stated to the two women. "Don't push Daphne in front of the press."

"I won't make that mistake again," Alanna grumbled.

"And, Daph, you need to respect your mother's career just as you want her to respect yours."

Like a reprimanded child, Daphne stared at the ground and said, "I won't be mean to the press anymore. Or bad mouth your choice in careers."

"This might be crazy but, what if…?" Miguel raised an eyebrow at the two ladies.

"Oh, no. Bad idea." Daphne shook her head wildly before Miguel had even finished his sentence.

And this only served to make Alanna more curious. "What? What's crazy?"

"What if you came with us, Alanna, as we worked to solve the murder of Amber Daniel?"

Alanna clapped and said, "I'd love to," at the same time Daphne stated flatly, "Absolutely not."

12.

It was over a heaping plate of tacos prepared by Mrs. Alvarez that Daphne told Miguel, "She's going to be a distraction. How do you think you'll be able to interview a suspect with them drooling all over my mom?"

With little hope of continuing the conversation with Amber's ghost after Alanna had so rudely scared her away, Miguel had coaxed the two women inside. It hadn't taken long before food was presented as the solution to all the problems in the world.

Miguel smiled and wiped his face with his napkin. "We'll just say she's researching a role."

"Oh, I've done that before." Alanna's face lit up. "I was playing the mayor of a small town with lots of strange occurrences happening. I followed around a real mayor for a whole day." She frowned. "It was really boring."

Daphne groaned.

Miguel reached over and squeezed her hand. "I just think you both could learn a little something about the other's life, that's all. If your mom got the chance to see you work, she'd understand why you're so passionate."

Daphne grunted. She knew deep in her heart that Alanna wouldn't actually be more than a minor distraction. She could see it in her mind's eye. But her decades of finding her mother's frivolity to be painful to watch couldn't be erased with one invitation from Miguel.

But she couldn't argue with his logic either.

He said they should try to understand each other and, dammit, he wasn't wrong. In all their years of knowing one another neither of them had ever even tried to put herself in the other's shoes. She may not like it. It might even be a long, painful, torturous process. But it could also be the path to peace between mother and daughter.

"So, when do we leave?" Alanna asked with a huge smile, as if they were talking about a new script and not someone's actual murder.

"More importantly, who are we talking to?" Miguel asked Daphne.

"His name is Barrett Thomas. He was a truck driver with some company named Dynamite Trucking, apparently out of Northern California. It probably won't surprise you to know that he was older than Amber and she had dumped Mike for him." Daphne let it all out with one gust.

Miguel raised an eyebrow. "That's a motive for Mike. Are we positive he didn't kill her?"

Daphne shook her head. "She knew her killer and I saw her death. It wasn't Mike who struck her in Roeding Park."

"Oh!" Alanna exclaimed with a wrist pressed to her forehead. "How gruesome."

Daphne glared at her before saying. "If you are going to be tagging along, you'll have to keep your exclamations to yourself."

"Okay, so we're looking for this Barrett guy. Amazing how easy you make this." Miguel smiled and took a huge bite of a taco.

"I don't think so." Daphne shook her head. "It's been forty years so he could be anywhere in the United States by now and he could have changed his name. But more importantly...."

Miguel watched her closely. "What?"

"There's more. Something about that necklace. Someone has it and that person is involved somehow. I'm just not sure exactly how," Daphne explained.

Miguel swore under his breath. "Always the damned necklace. We gotta find that thing." He fished his phone out of his pocket and pressed the call to Victoria De La Torre. The conversation was brief and his eyes were locked with Daphne's the whole time.

When Miguel hung up, Daphne didn't wait for his

update to announce, "The necklace isn't with the body."

Miguel nodded. "The killer has it, I guess."

Daphne shook her head. "Barrett is the killer. I have no doubt. But someone else has the necklace, and they're linked somehow."

"So Barrett had an accomplice?" Miguel asked. It wasn't unheard of, two people working together to bring about the demise of another. It was just unusual in a crime of passion, as this one seemed to be. "But if he killed her in a jealous rage, it doesn't sound premeditated."

The feeling of happiness washed over her and Daphne knew it was the sentiment that the accomplice had experienced. "Maybe not. But that someone wasn't too sad when she died." Another flash of someone burying Amber in the park. Daphne spoke mostly to herself as she stated, "That person watched and then buried her. Barrett killed her and ran. Someone else disposed of her body."

"And swiped the necklace," Miguel added.

"And took the necklace," Daphne agreed.

"A necklace? Now we're talking about things I know something about," Alanna added. "What kind of necklace are we talking?"

"A diamond necklace. A family heirloom," Daphne explained. She knew her mother was right about one thing: she can't help with murder, but she can help with jewelry.

Alanna nodded. "If it was well taken care of, antique jewelry can fetch quite the price. Do we know how many carats?"

Daphne held up her fingers about a half an inch apart to indicate size. "About this big sitting on her chest."

Alanna whistled, low and slow. "Oh, honey. That's five carats. We're talking well over a hundred thousand dollars. People have killed for less."

Alanna casually took a bite out of her taco, but Miguel shot up out of his chair. He looked directly at Daphne, positive she'd have all the answers. "Is that the real motive? Greed?"

Daphne took a deep breath and allowed her mind to open to the truths of Amber's story. "Someone wanted her gone. But they also wanted personal gain. So who profited from her death?"

Miguel again fished his phone from his pocket, barely waiting for the phone to be answered on the other end before blurting out what was on his mind. "Gina. Meet me at HQ. Daphne just spoke to Amber and we have more details."

"We're not even close to finished compiling the list of all her possible boyfriends." Gina paused for a moment. "Are you telling me that doesn't matter?"

"It might matter. But right now we need to switch tactics." Miguel started for the front door, indicating for Daphne and Alanna to follow. "We need to trace the necklace. Gina, that's what the killer was after. It's worth more than a hundred grand."

"Holy baby," was Gina's response. "That's quite the payout."

"So, if it was done at a pawn shop, there'd be a record. And it would most definitely stand out with a price that high," Miguel added, opening the front door to his childhood home.

"On it. I'll see what Spencer can dig up while we head back to the office." He could hear Gina getting in her car on the other end of the line. "Forty years and the asshole thinks he got away with it. Let's get that bastard."

"We're going to, Gina. I can sense it." Miguel looked at Daphne. "And then we're going to give that poor girl's soul some much deserved rest."

Daphne leaned up and kissed Miguel's cheek as he ended his call with Gina. "I love that you're thinking about the ghosts now."

Miguel smiled. "I always did. I just never took it quite so literally before you." Over his shoulder he called, "Heading out now, Ma!"

And without waiting for an answer, Daphne and Miguel rushed out the front door with an exuberance

Alanna didn't feel. She followed them anyway.

The sun was shining and cutting through the winter chill of the Central Valley. From the corner of the yard, Amber's ghost watched them leaving.

She locked eyes with Daphne as Miguel pulled out and began the drive back to the Fresno Police Department building downtown. She could feel it. Her soul knew after all these decades. She would finally find peace.

And Daphne was the key.

13.

"Holy shit! Alanna Savage?" Gina didn't even try to play it cool. Her jaw was slack the moment she laid eyes on the Hollywood star.

Which boosted Alanna's ego immensely and she smiled with her chin in the air. Ghosts and murders? She was useless. But fan girls? This was her element. This is where Alanna could really shine.

But Daphne didn't want to waste precious moments of Amber's afterlife boosting her mother's ego. She waved an arm dismissively near Alanna. "Pay her no attention. She's just tagging along. Pretend she's not even here."

But it was Daphne that Gina ignored as she ran to Alanna and gripped her hand in both of her own. "I've never met a movie star before. You are much prettier than I would have expected. And taller too."

Alanna beamed. "I get that a lot."

Not to be left out, Sheffley came up behind Gina for his own sneak peek at the celebrity in their midst. He stammered, "I...I... loved *Witch Doctor*. You were so good. Very believable. I can't believe you didn't win an award for that performance."

Alanna soaked it all in, her pride giving her a buoyancy that lifted her to the balls of her feet. "That's so kind of you to say. You know those award shows are all fixed. They collude to choose the winners. It means much more to me that someone like you thinks I'm deserving."

Daphne knew her mother was full of shit. Her ego was wounded from being snubbed at the award shows time and time again. But she didn't want to out her, so she folded her arms and huffed instead. "Are we done now? My mom can continue making useless art after we find Amber's killer."

"Daphne." Miguel chastised her, reminding her

that she and her mother were supposed to be learning to respect one another.

Old habits die hard.

"No, no. I agree. I am here to soak it all in for an upcoming role." Alanna winked at Sheffley as if he were in on some big bullshit secret. "Please do what you do. Pay me no mind."

"Well, if you're going to be playing a homicide detective, you should come sit by me. I'm the only lady cop in the room." Gina gestured at the seat beside her own at the conference table. Alanna sat next to her and began to rifle through all the papers and photos from the Amber Daniel case that were still strewn across the table.

When everyone had grabbed seats, Miguel decided it was time to brief the team. "We got the name of the killer. A boyfriend named Barrett Thomas."

Gina sat bolt upright in her seat. "What? Why didn't you mention that? Let's go get him."

"Because that's not all." Daphne leaned across the table. "When I had the dream that I watched

Amber's murder, I was sensing someone's point of view. Barrett lashed out that night, but there was someone watching who wanted Amber dead. And wanted her necklace."

"Barrett killed and ran, dumping the body. The accomplice is who cleaned up after him," Miguel explained.

"It has to be the DJ, right? If jealousy and finances are a motive, he's the obvious suspect?" Sheffley looked around the table for someone to agree with him. "The guy was an everyday party host and now he lives in a mansion."

"Possible," Miguel agreed. "But he also had means to earn his money legitimately. We'd need Daphne to confirm if he's lying." He turned to face her as he mentioned her name, winking at her as he did.

"So let me get Spencer in here. See if he's found the pawn shop yet," Gina proposed.

Miguel nodded. "I think the necklace is the key."

"So, are we still thinking it's one of her

boyfriends?" Sheffley asked. "We were able to find the names of five young men she was close with."

"Were you able to see the person watching the murder, Daphne?" Gina asked the blonde sitting across from her.

Daphne shook her head. "Not yet. In my dream, I was the accomplice, so it looked like me."

"I got your text, Gina." Spencer burst into the room in a disheveled T-shirt with some unknown stain all over the front. His clothes were wrinkled and his hair was every which way, like a mirror image to Daphne's wild style. "I found three possible pawn shops with expensive necklace purchases around the time of the murder."

"Any near Roeding Park?" Sheffley asked.

Miguel shook his head. "That doesn't necessarily mean anything. It could have been months before the perp sold the necklace."

"This one's downtown." Spencer handed a printout to Miguel. "Necklace was bought from the pawner for five thousand dollars."

Alanna was radiating at the mere idea of being asked an important question. "Way too low if we're talking a five-carat family heirloom."

"Oh, I didn't know it was five carat." Spencer looked through the printouts, scanning for the necklace size. "The biggest was two carats." He snatched back the printout from Miguel and announced, "Back to work. I'll keep looking for a larger diamond."

"Expand the timeframe too, Spencer," Miguel instructed. "It could have been a decade later."

"And, Spence," Gina called out just before he reached the conference room door. "Can you please track down a Barrett Thomas? He may be using an alias. We need an address for him."

"Okay. What's his story?"

"He's the killer." Daphne's eyes narrowed as she remembered the brutal way he'd beaten young Amber to death.

"The ghost told you?" Spencer didn't hide his shock. "Crazy. Necklace and Barrett Thomas. I'm on it!"

With a swirl of energy that matched his entrance, Spencer the tech guy vacated the room.

"That kid is so adorable." Alanna smiled and Daphne just rolled her eyes.

"What if…?" Gina looked at Daphne as she proffered her idea. "What if the mastermind never wanted the money?"

"What do you mean?" Miguel asked his partner, arms folded across his chest.

Gina shook her head. "I don't know. What if that person wanted her dead, but the necklace was just a memento or something?"

Sheffley scoffed. "You mean like a serial killer?"

"You don't have to be a serial killer to want a trophy of something you're proud of," Gina explained.

"It's weird," Daphne blurted. "I know they really wanted that necklace. But the murder? I can't sense why they would feel the need to kill her for a necklace. You could just steal it. Why does she have to die?"

"You know." Alanna was smiling. It annoyed

Daphne yet again that Alanna treated this like one big movie set. "Money is a powerful motive. But so is jealousy. I was in a movie once with a love triangle. The old boyfriend was furious at me for having a new love interest. The jealousy led to anger which led to murder." She clutched her chest at the memory. "I was horrified at the confrontation. Really challenged my emotional library."

"Mom. Please stop." Daphne held up a hand, embarrassed yet again that her mother was even here.

"Actually, Daph, she makes a good point. The necklace might have just been a bonus." Miguel walked over to Daphne.

"Back to the DJ. He was just dumped so he had a reason to be jealous. And the bonus of coming into a lot of money." Sheffley tapped an index finger on the table. "He's looking very guilty right now."

"We can look into DJ Bendy's career. Find out when he came into his money and if there's a paper trail for all of it," Gina proposed.

But Miguel shook his head. "I don't think we'll need to go that far." He grabbed Daphne's hand and pulled her up. "I didn't sense anything suspicious when I spoke to him, but Daphne might."

"Finally!" Daphne announced. "I've been waiting all day to see if that guy is telling the truth."

"I thought you had been on your way to see him earlier? What happened?" Gina asked Miguel and Daphne.

But it was Alanna that answered. "Daphne got into a run-in with the press. It's all over the internet."

"I'm sorry. What?" Gina's eyes widened at the ridiculous story she was being told.

But Daphne didn't flinch. "Nosey gossip columnists, all of them. I regret nothing. They don't have any right to butt into my private life."

Gina huffed a laugh. "But why would they feel a need to butt into your private life? Did I miss something?"

Gina zeroed in on Miguel who had the decency to

look embarrassed at the announcement he'd been withholding.

But it was Alanna who answered. "It's a by-product of being my daughter." She shrugged. "Naturally they're curious about the wedding of my only child."

Sheffley slapped Miguel on the back and said, "Congratulations, man." And Miguel accepted it warmly.

But Gina stood up with fire in her eyes. "You two are getting married and I hear about it from Daphne becoming an internet meme?!"

Daphne stood up to match her. "Gina. No one was keeping anything from anyone. We haven't set a date or anything. Miguel's mom called my mom and my mom attracts the press like flies. That's it."

Gina pursed her lips and turned her head to Alanna. "I thought you were here researching a role in a movie."

Alanna smiled and shrugged to neither confirm nor deny.

"Can we just refocus here?" Daphne shouted to anyone and everyone. "There's a girl who was murdered forty years ago, a murderer on the loose and a mastermind who thinks they've gotten away with it all. Our wedding will happen in due time, and you're all invited!" Her chest heaved with the exertion of shouting at the members in the room.

A heavy silence filled the room like a weighted blanket. And then Sheffley said, "I'm honored to be invited, Daphne."

Daphne nodded to Sheffley and then stormed out of the room.

Miguel laughed to himself. "It's been one heck of a day."

14.

"I know it might seem strange, our relationship." Alanna turned to Miguel in the front seat of his car. "But there's more there than meets the eye."

Miguel turned out of the parking lot, driving to pick Daphne up from the front of the downtown police headquarters, a beautiful building made almost completely of glass. She'd wanted a moment to cool down and Miguel understood.

Daphne may not handle everything the same way he would, but he knew her intentions were pure. She cared about justice for Amber, and that was all any of them wanted. And he knew the wedding was just a formality. Their bond was strong regardless of the legal paperwork that would declare it.

"I understand," Miguel told Alanna. And he did.

He wasn't just telling her what she wanted to hear. He knew Daphne well enough to know that her impatience with her mother had a lot more to do with the pressures she put on herself. "May I ask why you never had any other children."

He tensed, wondering whether this would strike a nerve with Alanna, but she seemed to take a moment to think about the answer. It was as if this aging star had never really had anyone to talk to about these things. As if no one had ever thought to ask her.

"Beck and I were really in love when Daphne was born." Alanna stared off into the distance as she recalled those happier days. "I could have had ten kids the way I felt in the early days, holding her in my arms with my handsome successful husband at my side." She sighed. "It's easy to look back on life and see where everything fell apart. But back then? I thought we were in a fairytale that would never end."

She paused at the memories and Miguel took this opportunity to squeeze her hand. She smiled, appreciating the gesture, and then continued. "But the infidelity was taxing and honestly brought out my own insecurities with getting older." And then Alanna let out an uncomfortable laugh. "And Daphne wasn't exactly the easiest child to rear. So, I guess the short answer is life." She nodded, satisfied with her answer. "Life is the reason I never had more children."

Miguel pulled up in front of the glass building, smiling at Daphne standing there in a long black skirt and disheveled hair. "I get that. There are just some things you can't plan for."

Alanna followed his gaze and laughed. "She's not for everyone, for sure. But you two make it work somehow."

Daphne climbed in the car with a scowl as Alanna said to Miguel, "I can see why you're a good detective. You make people want to talk to you."

Daphne looked from Miguel to Alanna and asked, "What did I miss?"

Miguel smiled at Daphne in the rearview mirror.

"Can't a man and his future mother-in-law have a few secrets between them?"

Daphne groaned and folded her arms across her chest. "Not in *this* car." And then she added, "But I won't ever mention again that you got my mom to open up about my dad's cheating. Not his finest quality." She softened a bit, looking at two people who were important in her life, getting along and smiling. She rarely saw her mother smile, especially not lately, and especially not when it came to Beck Winters. Daphne recognized the relief that Alanna had expressed in opening up to Miguel and felt thankful he could be there for her mother in a way she never could. And certainly never would. "Thank you, by the way. For treating my mom like a person."

Miguel half-smiled at the two beautiful blondes he was chauffeuring. "She is a person."

"This is nice." Alanna beamed in the front seat, her beautiful full blonde locks resting perfectly on her shoulder. "We're like a normal family. I could get used to this."

Daphne scowled. She wanted to tell her mother not to get used to it. To tell her that she wasn't welcome and that Daphne couldn't wait for her to leave. But the truth was that while they were sitting in the car working together on something that meant so much to Daphne, having normal conversations, she liked it too.

So she said nothing.

Miguel locked eyes with her in the rearview mirror and smiled. Daphne just shook her head. He swore he wasn't psychic, but in those moments she found it hard to believe. When it came to Daphne's innermost thoughts and feelings, Miguel was tuned in to her in a way she could only describe as sensitive. He absolutely could read her mind. So if that wasn't psychic, she wasn't sure how the word was defined.

"Shall we go drill the DJ, my ladies?" Miguel asked, still staring at Daphne in the mirror.

"Yes, let's," came the bubbly reply from the front seat.

Daphne shook her head at Miguel, but she smiled

back at him in the mirror. She wasn't mad at Miguel. It was true that his intuition with her made her feel exposed in an uncomfortable way, but she had gotten past that. She knew that he was always on her side.

And weirdly, she knew her mother was too. Alanna may be ignorant and vapid, but she had never been openly hostile toward Daphne.

As Miguel pulled out into traffic, Alanna shifted in her seat so she could speak to both Miguel and Daphne. "So when exactly is this wedding I am helping put together? We never really did get the chance to talk about it."

Daphne groaned so Miguel responded for the both of them. "It's a bit of a sore subject with Daphne. That's why she lost her cool with Gina and Sheffley."

Alanna clicked her tongue. "She's always blown things like this out of proportion."

Daphne leaned forward, feeling her face get hot again. "I'm sitting right here and I do no such thing."

Alanna shifted uncomfortably in her seat to look

at her daughter. "You have convinced yourself that celebrations and parties are a waste of time. And yes, when it's just Hollywood people getting together to brown-nose, you may have a point. But you can't throw the baby out with the bath water, Daphne Lorraine Savage Winters. People like to celebrate love and marriage." She turned back around to face front. "It gives them hope."

"Oh, yeah?" Daphne raised her voice. "Well, for your information I was looking forward to a wedding and reception. I just didn't want to make it all about you and dad. I wanted one day to actually be about me!"

Daphne knew she sounded childish, but she didn't even care.

There was a moment of silence before Alanna responded, "I'm sorry, Daphne. I'm sorry I tipped the press and made it about me. I guess I can now see that it was rude to upstage the bride."

Daphne tightened her lips, a snotty retort sitting on the tip of her tongue. But she held it, knowing that there was no reason to not soak this moment in with all its glory. Her mother had never apologized to her in her life. "Thank you."

Miguel looked at her again in the rearview mirror. "And I'm sorry, too, that I didn't know your middle name was Lorraine. That's pretty."

Alanna smiled too. "It was my grandmother's name. The woman who raised me."

"Grandma Lorraine is the best. She practically raised me too." Daphne smiled, her previous attitude beginning to float away.

"Oh? You've never mentioned that. Did she live with you in Malibu?" Miguel asked.

Alanna shook her head. "No, she died a decade before Daphne was born."

"I should've known." Miguel half-smiled. "So, Grandma Jean?"

"My dad's side," Daphne explained, knowing that Miguel had met her spirit while they were finding Maddy. Had seen her ghost even at the séance in Duncan's crappy apartment. "And, yes, it was Grandma Lorraine."

Miguel nodded in understanding as Daphne answered his unasked question.

But Alanna was completely unable to follow the unspoken conversation. "What? What was my grandmother?" The edge of panic lacing her tone made Daphne laugh.

"Nothing bad, mom. Miguel wondered where I got my gift of sight." Daphne locked eyes with Miguel's reflection. "And it was Grandma Lorraine. She was psychic too."

And now it was Alanna's turn to laugh. "That's ridiculous. My grandmother? She was practically an extra on *Leave it to Beaver*. The classic stay-at-home mom from yesteryear. Strait-laced and obedient."

Daphne nodded. "And psychic. She taught me everything she knew."

Alanna swallowed the jealousy and it became anger when it combined with the lump in her throat. "She never said anything to me. Why did she exclude me from that part of her life?"

Daphne rolled her eyes before responding with a tone that matched Alanna's in raised emotion. "Because. You don't share this gift. You hate it even. Why would she open up about it? So you could judge her?"

Alanna pursed her lips and took a moment to respond. "I don't hate your gift. I just didn't enjoy the honesty that it brought. Sometimes it's easier to live with dark secrets staying buried." She turned to Miguel with a sad smile. "Ignorance really is bliss, after all."

But Daphne didn't agree with that philosophy. At all.

Only now that she was an adult, however, she understood the pain that it brought for her mother. When she was living with Alanna, she never took the moment to realize—or care, more likely—that announcing people's transgressions wasn't always without its side-effects. Especially when plopped before them like a steaming turd.

"Well," Daphne retorted, "the truth is going to

come out one way or another. So, you either swallow it and it eats you from inside like it did to Grandma Lorraine, who chose to take one for the team because decorum called for it." She leaned back against the seat back with a force that felt good thudding against her back. "Or you release it into the atmosphere and take everyone out with you like a bomb. Which was always more my approach."

"I remember," was all Alanna could say.

Daphne, for once, chose her next words more carefully than she normally would. Perhaps for the first time in her life she felt a pang of sensitivity toward her mother's plight. She had truly loved Beck Winters and had been wounded by the betrayal. Add to it the joy of a society that prefers its women perpetually twenty-five, and she knew her mother had pain that ran deep.

Everyone had their coping mechanisms. Alanna's was to ignore it just as her mother had taught her. And Daphne's was to call people on their shit. Two paths to the same mountain: trying to ease the hurt that wounded your soul.

"If you never knew about the affairs, it wouldn't make them go away. You took back control of your life because he couldn't abuse you in secret. Ignorance isn't bliss, mom. It's delayed torture."

Alanna smiled but it was laced with sadness.

Miguel knew the mother and daughter were finally getting somewhere, but even he could sense the ambience in the room getting thick with emotion. "Let's play some music, shall we?" And he turned on the radio to the first station with a song he recognized.

No one spoke anymore as they drove to DJ Bendy's house.

When they pulled up to the palatial home in Northwest Fresno, Daphne and Alanna marveled at its size and grandeur.

"Please don't take offense at this." Alanna spoke in wonder. "But I didn't even know homes like this existed in Fresno."

"It's definitely how the other half lives," Miguel

said as he began to climb out of the car.

"Nope," Daphne announced. "He had nothing to do with it."

"Geez, Daph." Miguel huffed a laugh. "You haven't even laid eyes on the guy."

"Your instincts were right the first time. You should stop second-guessing your gut, Miguel. You are more intuitive than you think." Daphne waved a finger at him. "Mike Benton was in love with Amber and was truly heartbroken when she called it off and then went missing, denying him the opportunity to win back her affections, which is all he ever wanted. Wants still, if he's being honest with himself."

"But the necklace?" Miguel asked.

Daphne shook her head. "Not him."

"Mind if I ask him a few questions, since we've come all this way?" Miguel asked.

Daphne curled her lip. "If you want to waste your time, be my guest."

"And will you be waiting in the car, then?"

Miguel raised an eyebrow at his fiancée.

"I'm going in. I've always wanted to witness an interrogation." Alanna slammed the door with finality as she followed Miguel out of the car.

"He's not actually a suspect," Miguel laughed.

"He's not anything. Just collateral damage from a terrible crime that happened forty years ago," Daphne shouted out the window as she folded her arms across her chest and flopped back against the seat to emphasize how much of a waste of time talking to DJ Bendy would be.

But the debate ended when Miguel's phone rang.

"Detective Alvarez," Miguel answered.

"It's Spencer," the tech's voice came through the line. "We found him. Barrett Thomas. He still uses his real name."

"Unbelievable."   Miguel shook his head. This Barrett guy was either really arrogant or not too bright. "Get someone to bring him in. I can finish the paperwork when I get back. This guy's a murderer and we need him off the streets."

"No need. He's in Dublin Pen. Picked up for armed robbery and assault, and as a convicted felon in possession of a firearm."

Miguel let out a breath of air. "Sounds about right."

Spencer couldn't argue. "Want me to tell them you'll swing by when you're done interviewing Bendy?"

"Nah." He locked eyes with Daphne. "I have it on good authority that the DJ is innocent. Just a man who fell in love with a murder victim."

Spencer laughed. "Good authority. Daphne will love that title."

After they hung up, Daphne climbed out of the car and kissed Miguel's cheek.

"What's that for?" Miguel asked.

Daphne shrugged. "Spencer's right. I like being a good authority."

"So, if we're not interviewing the DJ, what's next?" Alanna asked. She was still bouncing with the thrill of the investigation she had no right to be involved with.

Miguel put an arm around Daphne. "Federal Prison up in Dublin, California. It's the home address of one Barrett Thomas."

"I know of a way to get every answer we need." Daphne looked at her mother and then at her fiancée. There was no twinkle in her eye. It was a stare of determination and stubbornness. "I'll have to go in."

Alanna laughed. "Go in? The prison? Are you insane?"

Daphne shook her head. "No. Even worse."

But before she could explain, Miguel was already shaking his head and protesting. "No way. Absolutely not. It's not safe for you to constantly be going in and out of criminal minds."

"What?!" Alanna couldn't even act her way out of the shock that took control of her. "What on earth does that mean?"

"I don't just talk to ghosts, mom," Daphne

explained with a roll of her eyes. "I'm psychic. I can get inside people's heads." And then she quickly added, "When I need to."

"So, you can see their thoughts and memories and stuff?" Alanna gasped.

"She can even control their actions. Make them tell the truth and such." Miguel turned to Daphne. "But she's not doing it. It takes too much of a toll."

"I'll admit I'm novice at this particular skill," Daphne responded honestly. "But we're talking about solving a forty-year-old murder and closure for a family who has suffered all this time."

Alanna surprised Daphne by sweeping her up into a bear hug. "That's incredible, Daphne. You are like a superhero. I'm so impressed."

Daphne was taken aback by the words and the gesture, so she just stood in shock, her arms limp at her side, while her estranged mother squeezed her tight.

And when her mother pulled back, Daphne surprised Miguel and Alanna with a revelation of her own. "I can do this, but I do think I need some pointers. Which is why I've been working with Anne Marie Marinovich."

"Who?" Alanna asked.

But Miguel knew the name. "Anne Marie Marinovich with the FBI?"

"That would be the one," Daphne confirmed.

"I don't get it." Alanna looked from Daphne to Miguel. "What would someone in the FBI be doing working with a psychic?"

"She's a well-known criminal profiler," Miguel explained. "Super famous in the law enforcement community for nailing details that no one else could even think of. Like all the way down to the name of the company the criminal works for and things like that."

Daphne nodded. "Because she's psychic. And she gets in people's heads and then pulls out information."

"So she's been training you to get better at digging in people's minds?" Miguel didn't even bother hiding his surprise.

"Cayman gave me her name. They're old friends. After everything that went down with Stryker in the Maddy Laurens case, he thought she might be a good resource for me."

Miguel whistled. "Unbelievable. Why didn't you mention it until now?"

Daphne shrugged again. "Didn't really have a reason to until now. But before we go to Dublin to dig through Barrett Thomas's mind, I think we should get some guidance from Anne Marie. Just to be safe."

"So is this going to be a thing now?" Miguel had to ask.

"I can help more people this way," Daphne explained.

Alanna climbed back in the car, encouraging Miguel and Daphne to follow. "Don't even bother trying to talk her out of it, Miguel. If it's between saving people and virtually anything else, she always makes the same choice."

But Miguel didn't need to be told that. He kissed Daphne's forehead, and with no words at all they exchanged the one philosophy in life that they both shared. A need for justice so deep in their inner cores that digging for a lifetime could never uncover the roots. Miguel knew it. And he was reminded yet again that his urge to protect Daphne was unfounded. She was strong in ways he couldn't even understand. And he loved her for it.

Daphne smiled, knowing everything he felt without his having to voice it. "Take me to Anne Marie's."

15.

Anne Marie Marinovich was a tough woman.

She had spent a lifetime profiling the worst of the worst for the FBI, and it had taken any soft parts of her psyche and crusted them over into a shell of an exterior. She had seen some things. Horrific things. Things she couldn't even describe to her fellow law enforcement officers because there were no words.

She had been trained not to trust anyone. People were psychopaths, murderers, crooked as a question mark. Yes, she had the ability to look into their souls and see that not everyone was that way, but since she only dug around in the minds of the worst society had to offer, she had become brainwashed to the belief that what she witnessed was the majority, not the minority.

So she had locked herself away in her retirement, refusing to see people unless she absolutely had to.

She had purchased a cabin in the hills on the way to Yosemite National Park. Her closest neighbor was miles away and she only went into town if she was out of something crucial. If Daphne was blunt, Anne Marie was sharp as a dagger. Caustic. Spiteful even.

But for some reason even she couldn't explain, Anne Marie had taken a liking to Daphne.

When she had gotten the message a few minutes ago that Daphne was on her way, she had even been shocked to find her lips turning upward in something resembling a smile.

She knew her reputation in law enforcement was surrounded by myth and legend. Rumors swirled about all her abilities and superhuman talents. She never corrected any of them, enjoying the fantasy that people built in their own minds about how someone could be so right all the time.

Anne Marie would just shrug and smile, as if

knowing random details of a serial killer were something you could learn in night classes.

With her dark hair pulled up into a tight bun, Anne Marie stood at the window waiting for the one person, the only other person she knew of, who could actually understand her life and her secrets. Daphne even seemed to respect her need for withdrawing from society.

And Daphne had the same talents Anne Marie had.

Her protégé might even be better than she was at her age. And certainly Anne Marie had had no one to coach her, guide her. Daphne could one day be catching people before they even committed the crime.

But this was exhausting work, and Anne Marie didn't miss it at all.

As the dark sedan pulled into her long, curving driveway, she watched it with a secret satisfaction.

But her joy turned bitter when she saw three people climb out of the car. She stormed to the front door of her cabin and stood there scowling.

Daphne wasn't expecting a greeting or a warm reception, so she just marched through the front door without a care. But Miguel and Alanna could sense the animosity.

"Uh. Shall we just wait in the car?" Miguel asked

"Yes," Anne Marie snapped.

And this made Daphne laugh, giving her the most joy she'd felt all day. "Anne Marie, this is my mother, and this is my fiancée, Miguel, the cold case detective I was telling you about."

"Hi, I am Alanna Savage." Alanna marched forward with her hand extended. It went unshaken. "I'm researching a role."

"Bullshit," was all Anne Marie responded.

Daphne laughed again. "She's psychic, mom. Remember?"

"Oh, yes. That's right." Alanna leaned in and whispered, "You're not going to go poking around inside my brain, are you?"

Daphne braced herself for comments about the emptiness Anne Marie may find, or how her mere existence was a waste of human flesh. But Anne Marie simply responded, "I'm retired."

"They're harmless, I assure you. And we'll be quick." Daphne once again marched in and made herself at home in the small front room with the potbelly stove. Miguel and Alanna followed uncomfortably.

Miguel took a chance to say, "If I may, Ms. Marinovich, your reputation in law enforcement proceeds you. I'm honored to get the chance to work with you."

Her face held no warmth, but she nodded in response, as if this were the sort of greeting she'd expect from a fellow law enforcement professional. "Call me Anne Marie."

"Yes, ma'am. Anne Marie, ma'am," Miguel stuttered awkwardly. Something about this stone-faced woman who could also read your thoughts was greatly intimidating.

"I need your help," Daphne said to her mentor.

"He's not the worst you've faced, by any means," Anne Marie announced as she made herself comfortable on the recliner by the front window.

Miguel noticed how opposite these two women appeared on the exterior, despite having so much in common. Daphne looked like someone who had rolled out of bed and grabbed the first skirt she'd found crumpled on the ground. Anne Marie was dressed in a pressed pantsuit that looked like she could still be called on a case for the FBI at any moment.

But their souls were kindred.

"I'm not scared he'll hurt me," Daphne snorted.

"Did I ever tell you about the Black Widow Killer case I worked on? Must've been about twenty years ago." Anne Marie shook her head at the memory. "This bitch thought she had outsmarted everyone. A real old-fashioned narcissist. But just from watching the initial interview after her fourth husband died under mysterious circumstances, I knew she had done it. I knew how she had done it and everything. Not even a challenge."

Miguel nodded. "Daphne does that too. She just knows things."

Anne Marie sighed. "But I didn't stop there. I should've. We had her. She was going to prison for the rest of her life. What made me dig inside her memories? What compelled me to share the thoughts of one of the most sadistic people I had ever encountered?"

"I get it, Anne Marie." Daphne shook her head. "You think I'll get addicted to going into people's heads. But I won't. I don't enjoy it."

"Daphne, I *hated* it." Anne Marie leaned back. "And I did it anyway. Every time."

"Then that settles it." Miguel reached a hand out for Daphne's. "Let's just go. We can interrogate Barrett Thomas without you having to do this."

"But the thing is," Anne Marie continued, keeping her eyes on Daphne. "The thing is I found six other murders she had committed. Unsolved ones that probably would have gone unsolved forever. I knew everything she had done in her whole life. How she'd done it and how she'd gotten away with it."

Miguel let his hand fall to his side.

"Give me some pointers. Show me how to protect myself," Daphne pleaded with her mentor.

"I wasn't accusing you of getting addicted to reaching into people's minds. I'm afraid you'll get addicted to chasing one more case. Solving one more crime. Finding justice one more time." Anne Marie scowled as she and Daphne spoke to one another, Alanna and Miguel still uncomfortably watching.

Daphne frowned. She couldn't deny that one. "I have to help Amber rest in peace. She needs the truth to be known." After a pause she added, "You know you would do the same."

Anne Marie sighed. Of course she would. She always had until she couldn't anymore. "The trick is, get in and get out. Don't dwell even a minute longer than you need to."

"But what if he answers us from the start? What

if he tells the truth? Then she doesn't need to go in, right?" Miguel asked.

Anne Marie turned a cold stare to the investigator. "You're afraid of the wrong things, Detective. Those minds, especially minds like Barrett Thomas. Those minds are weak. They cannot harm Daphne. My guess is he won't even know she was in there." Anne Marie leaned back in her seat. "The Black Widow never knew how I got my information."

Miguel locked eyes with Daphne. "Then, dare I ask, what I *should* be afraid of?"

Daphne stared at the ground as Anne Marie stated, "Every time you dive into darkness, you take a little piece of it home with you. Over decades, imagine what that darkness does to your soul."

"What are we saying?" Miguel looked between the two psychic women. "Daphne? Are you going to turn evil?"

"Teach me how to stop it, Anne Marie," Daphne begged again.

"She won't turn evil," Anne Marie explained. "She'll become a beacon for evil. Darkness calls to darkness."

"Nope. Not happening. Let's go." Miguel reached for Daphne again, but she pushed his hand away.

"She's not surrounded by any evil spirits," Daphne explained to Miguel before turning back to Anne Marie. "So teach me what to do."

"Close your eyes," Anne Marie instructed, and Daphne obeyed. Miguel stood over her as if he were able to physically swoop in and save her from her own psychic visions. "When you see the murder of Amber Daniel, tell me what you see."

The moment Daphne closed her eyes, she was instantly back there. The cold, crisp night air. The smell of wet wood and pine. The car parked across the parking lot. She was able to see from the bushes where she was hiding and watching. "I see the park. Lots of trees. He's hitting her. She's screaming and fighting back, but it's futile. He climbs in the car and speeds away."

Daphne frowned at both the vision and the memory of the vision. She knew what happened next. She opened her eyes so she wouldn't have to see it again. "She's dead. I check on her, and she's lying there dead."

Anne Marie nodded, as if she had had the same vision and knew everything Daphne knew. "And what do you feel?"

Daphne made a sound somewhere between a snort and a tsk. "How do you think I feel? I feel awful. I just watched someone be killed."

Anne Marie pursed her lips. "I don't think that's all you feel."

"What are you saying?" Daphne had to ask.

But Anne Marie just shook her head. "There's something about that vision that feels important. Close your eyes again." Daphne hesitated for a brief second before obliging. "Now. Look at your feet."

"I'm wearing Keds. So?"

"Follow your feet as they run toward the victim," Anne Marie instructed.

Daphne sighed, but despite the fact that Anne Marie was pushing her in uncomfortable ways, she trusted her. Daphne knew that her end goal was the same as Daphne's. To get in, get the information, solve the case, and do it safely. Daphne followed the white Keds as they ran across the parking lot and saw Amber lying there, bloody in the moonlight. She had to swallow the bile at the sight.

"Stay with your feet," Anne Marie instructed.

It sounded like dumb advice, but she was willing to see this exercise through. Daphne watched as the feet stepped toward the dead girl, the white shoes a stark contrast to the red, pooling blood. Inside her head she was screaming at herself to run and get help. To call the police. Maybe, just maybe this bloody mess of a girl was still alive.

But her feet kept inching forward.

She watched as her knees bent over the body and her hand reached out toward the victim's throat. Daphne gasped, horrified, as she watched her own hand reach out and grab the diamond necklace dangling from Amber's throat. Blood or no blood, she watched her hand yank the necklace, breaking the chain, and stealing it.

Daphne's eyes opened wide at what she had just witnessed.

"Those weren't your feet," Anne Marie announced.

"They're hers." Daphne spoke barely above a whisper as she processed the vision.

"Of course, we know they aren't Daphne's feet," Alanna said, rolling her eyes. "She'd never be caught dead in Keds."

"Whose feet are they?" Miguel asked. He was feeding off Daphne's energy, knowing she had witnessed something shocking, but unable to fully understand.

"I was seeing through the eyes of the person who masterminded the whole thing. Whoever wanted her dead and whoever stole that necklace," Daphne explained, looking up at Miguel with determination in her eyes. "She was there that night, watching and waiting."

"So, it was a female perp? Wearing Keds?" Miguel asked.

"That should narrow your suspect pool to about five hundred thousand people in the greater Fresno area," Anne Marie said sarcastically.

But suddenly Daphne was happy. "This should be easy then. All I have to do is see who hired Barrett to kill Amber. That will come through his memories easily enough." She turned to her mentor. "Thank you for helping me push through."

"Let's start with interviewing him, though," Miguel again pleaded. "It was forty years ago. He's already in prison. What does he have to lose to tell the truth?"

"That's not the secret," Anne Marie announced as she stood up.

Miguel froze. "Then what is?"

"Here, Daphne." Anne Marie walked over to an end table near the window and opened a small drawer.

She pulled out a long, white candle with strange markings on it. "Burn this after any time you go into a criminal's mind. The positive energy will balance out the negative."

"That's it? That's all she has to do?" Miguel asked with a skeptical raise of his eyebrow.

Anne Marie stared him down. Hard. "This is thirty years of my trials and tribulations that I am handing down as wisdom." She spared a glance at Daphne. "It's about all I can do for her. Daphne is more skilled than I ever was. My only secret sauce was I never told anyone at the Bureau how I did it." She smiled but it was almost wicked in its glee. "They thought I was using advanced psychology."

"Then how did Detective Cayman know?" Miguel asked. "I mean, to introduce you two? He must've known something."

Anne Marie lifted her chin. "When someone else gets a reputation for never being wrong, let's just say oddballs have a way of finding each other. When I caught wind his rep was as good as mine, I may have done a little reconnaissance."

Daphne took the candle and squeezed Anne Marie's hand in both of hers as she did so. She knew a hug would be uncomfortable for them both. "Thank you, Anne Marie."

"So that's it?" Miguel asked again. "This candle is all she needs and she's safe? This feels like a text message or something, not really worthy of a face-to-face visit."

But Daphne and Anne Marie smirked before saying in unison, "It's a psychic thing."

Alanna rolled her eyes. "I actually think this lady is weirder than you, Daphne."

16.

The drive from Anne Marie Marinovich's isolated cabin in the mountains to the Federal Penitentiary in Dublin, California, was a quiet one. It was hard for Daphne to put into words the kindred spirit she felt with Anne Marie. There were very few people who understood her abilities and fewer still who could actually do what she did.

And Daphne had lived a lonely existence for much of her life because of this.

She'd resolved early in her life to be a weirdo and a freak, but knowing even just one person who used her psychic abilities to find justice just as Daphne did? That made her feel just a little bit more normal. And it soothed her soul.

But how could Miguel understand something like

that? She looked at his clean-cut clothes, slicked down hair all aligned, handsome face. He had had adversity in his life, just as everyone had. But he'd never been an outcast. The camaraderie of social discards was a stronger bond than the run-of-the-mill friendships of the socially accepted and popular. There was no way she could ever explain all that to Miguel.

And as usual, as if he could read her mind, he silently reached over and squeezed her hand.

"Grandma Lorraine did tell me a weird story once," Alanna suddenly blurted out from the back seat.

The disruption to Daphne's thoughts in such a disjointed way jarred Daphne. "What are you talking about?"

"I'm trying to reconcile the woman I knew with the psychic you claim she was," Alanna answered.

"I don't *claim* anything. She was psychic," Daphne retorted, folding her arms across her chest in finality.

"What was the story, Alanna?" Miguel asked in

an attempt to keep the peace. There may also have been a curiosity to know more about the woman that raised the two ladies in the car with him.

"Oh." Alanna responded, clearly surprised that anyone cared. "I had been on Hollywood sets since I was a child. My parents were both in the business, so I had grown up in that environment. But when I was about fourteen, Grandma Lorraine pulled me aside and told me not to pursue Hollywood and acting. She told me to consider other careers."

"Mom, that could have just been her way of getting you to consider all your options. How is that weird?" Daphne asked. Despite what it might have meant to Daphne's very existence, she couldn't deny that a part of her thought Grandma Lorraine had probably been imparting some very well-earned wisdom. And that her mother had been a fool not to listen.

"How did she know about Beck? How did she know my career would skyrocket, only to plummet a few years later?"

Daphne turned around from the front seat to look at her mom. "Do you even hear yourself? You're like a Hollywood cliché in every sense of the word. No one needs psychic powers to predict that eventuality."

Miguel tapped Daphne and then shook his head to warn her off when she caught his eye.

"Daphne, I'm telling you. She said it like she *knew*," Alanna argued back. "I didn't listen but of course her prediction was right." Alanna shrugged like the facts were all there in black and white. "I guess Grandma Lorraine was psychic."

"Well, I guess there's one thing we do agree on." Daphne flopped back in her seat, staring out the window.

"The rest of the world must seem like idiots." Miguel half-smiled at Daphne. "Since we can't see the future and know things as easily as you can."

"Sometimes," Daphne admitted. "But I don't think you need to be psychic to encourage someone to pursue all options when it comes to choosing a career."

Alanna heaved a heavy sigh. "It was all I'd ever

known, Daphne. There wasn't a single other thing I could imagine myself doing." She chuckled to herself. "And you have to admit, I'm good at it."

"And even I know you can't save people from themselves," Daphne muttered.

As they pulled into the expansive parking lot at the Dublin Federal Correctional Institution, they noticed many open spaces. But toward the narrow walkway that led to the front of the prison itself was a loan car that Daphne recognized instantly with no help from her psychic abilities. She knew who was there with them before they'd climbed out of the car.

"What's she doing here?" Daphne asked no one in particular.

"Who's here?" Miguel looked around, not noticing a single soul that would catch his attention.

"Anne Marie." Daphne frowned.

"Marinovich?" Miguel asked. "Who we just left in the mountains?"

"She must drive like a maniac because you're

pretty heavy footed, Miguel," Alanna stated from the backseat.

The car had barely ceased moving when Daphne was flying out of it. "What on earth are you doing here?"

Anne Marie was leaning against the back of her car, sunglasses on. "Same thing as you. I couldn't resist being a part of this case. Old habits die hard."

"You could've just come with us." Daphne gestured toward Miguel's car.

"Anne Marie." Miguel nodded in greeting toward the former profiler as he climbed out of the car. "Curious about what Barrett Thomas would say, huh?"

Alanna was a bit slower but followed suit in gathering at the back of Anne Marie's car.

Anne Marie shrugged. "This is a compelling cold case. And I'm addicted to justice. And the murderer isn't even the mastermind?" Anne Marie shook her head. "I'm intrigued."

"Well, I do appreciate that you can be here for Daphne, but I don't love that you were poking around in

Daphne's head for details." Miguel frowned.

"Don't be ridiculous. I would never." Anne Marie stood up straight. "She's far too strong for that anyway."

Miguel looked at Daphne and seemed placated. "Okay. Then how do you know all the details of the case?"

Anne Marie jutted out her chin. "I was in yours. And let me say, pretty dark memories in there, Detective."

At the look of shock and horror on Miguel's face, Daphne waved a hand between her mentor and her fiancée. "Okay, okay. Get in, get the name, get out. That's the plan with Barrett, right?"

"Yes," Anne Marie stated. "I suggest Detective Alvarez interview him per standard operating procedure. That will distract him while you dig around for what you need, Daphne."

Alanna giggled and all three of the others in the party glared in response.

"What could possibly be funny?" Anne Marie

tightened her lips like an admonishing old school marm.

"I just…" Alanna started laughing all the harder. "I really never thought I'd live to see the day when I had to deal with *two* of you people." She gestured between Daphne and Anne Marie. "You're just both so… unique."

Anne Marie turned a hard stare toward Alanna. "You people? Really?"

But this just made Alanna laugh harder. So, Anne Marie turned her glower toward Daphne. "Is this going to be happening all day? Because it's very distracting."

Daphne just shrugged. "Probably. For some odd reason my mom is uncomfortable with psychics, despite being raised by one and then raising one herself. Let's go."

Alanna was still giggling as they all marched into the federal prison.

The force of the negative emotion hit Daphne like a punch in the gut, and she stumbled backward in a physical recoil.

"I hate these places, too," Anne Marie responded

to Daphne's stumble. "Usually, I try to coordinate bringing the incarcerated to me so I can avoid the emotions. But every once in a while you just have to push through."

"In the business, we are taught to use the emotions. They help tell the story," Alanna explained, finally taking the whole thing more seriously.

"Not helpful, Mom," Daphne responded with tight lips.

Miguel checked his firearm and explained why they were there. They were then buzzed in and led down a long, sterile hallway. The few times Daphne had to tag along to visit inmates they were usually in public settings. But here they were led to a private room and it seemed classier somehow.

As if he could read her thoughts, Miguel said, "Federal Prisons often have rooms for inmates and their lawyers to meet privately. It's a budgetary thing not all prison systems have."

Daphne nodded and then took a seat at the small

metal table in the center of the room. The walls were cement and the one orange door had a small window. The floors looked like what Daphne remembered from her school cafeteria days, and the chair she sat in was plastic. If this was what the fancy budgets allowed, she figured they must splurge elsewhere.

"What's your role, Anne Marie?" Miguel asked the former FBI profiler.

Without making eye contact with him, Anne Marie answered coldly, "I'm just here for entertainment. I don't get out much."

Miguel would've laughed if it wasn't so true.

Another buzz and the single orange door opened with a correctional officer leading a man with a long, brown beard in a bright orange jumpsuit. Barrett Thomas was guided to the chair across from Daphne, and then a chain connected to his handcuffs was connected to a metal loop on the top of the table.

"Five minutes," was all the officer said before leaving the room and closing the door with another buzz behind him.

Barrett Thomas was barrel-chested and tall. His dark, hairy arms were covered in tattoos and his long hair was pulled back. The man before them neither looked malnourished nor lacking in exercise. This was a man who was flourishing in prison. Daphne had to take a deep breath to calm herself from the anger and violence flooding from him and threatening to drown her.

Daphne nodded to Miguel. She wasn't going in until Miguel was distracting him with the interrogation. Miguel took a seat next to Daphne while Alanna and Anne Marie remained standing in the back of the room.

"Barrett Thomas?" Miguel asked.

The inmate stuck out his chin and asked in return, "Anybody got a smoke?"

"You can't smoke in here," Miguel answered before continuing. "Mr. Thomas, we're here investigating the death of Melissa Amber Daniel from January of 1989. Her remains have just been located, and we know it was a homicide."

Barrett remained stoic. "So? People go missing every day."

"We know you were dating her," Miguel stated. Barrett neither confirmed nor denied. "Can you fill us in on the last time you saw her? When was it and what happened that day?"

Barrett shrugged his large shoulders. "What do you want to know?"

"Anything you can tell us that can help us make sense of her untimely death, Mr. Thomas," Miguel answered.

Daphne could sense that this man was not going to make any of this easy on them. Sure, he was already in prison, but confessing to a murder was still not high on anyone's priority list, inmate or not.

She stole a glance at Anne Marie, then a side eye at Miguel, and then dove into the mind of Barrett Thomas.

People had a vibe they exuded, similar to their aura, everyone's vibe being just a little bit different and unique. Daphne immediately sensed a very hard life as she dug around in Barrett's mind. Born into another life, this man might have made very different choices, been successful even. This wasn't a vapid, dark place but simply rough. That was the word that came into Daphne's mind. Barrett Thomas was rough.

Miguel continued asking questions and getting vague answers while Daphne pored through memories searching for his time with Amber. She saw an alcoholic abusive father and an absentee mother who left him at a young age. She saw him spending more time on the streets and then eventually escaping by learning to drive a truck.

And that's when he met Amber.

Daphne saw how he felt about her from the moment he saw her. He noticed her beauty and was drawn to her gentleness. Something about her calmed him and made him want to be a better person.

But deep inside of him was a need to destroy things that tried to calm him. And despite his love for

Amber, there was a looming resentment.

So, when Samantha showed up in his life, it was a far easier sell than it should have been for Barrett to turn on Amber.

Samantha was everything Amber wasn't. She was no great beauty, plain even. Amber had had so many things offered to her on a silver platter, and Samantha had had to scrape by just to survive. Samantha was bitter, jealous, angry, dark.

And she had wanted many things that Amber had, but none of them as much as she wanted Barrett.

Daphne watched as Samantha approached Barrett for the first time. She twirled her hair and smiled, but it did nothing for Barrett. He wasn't attracted to Samantha at all. Daphne stared at her dark brown hair, her nose too big for her face, her long skirt.

And white Keds on her feet.

Daphne gasped as she left Barrett's mind.

Barrett curled his lip as he stared across the interrogation table at the quirky blonde. "What's wrong with her?"

"Daphne? Everything okay?" Miguel asked.

"I know who the feet belonged to." Daphne turned in her seat to look back at Anne Marie. "It was Samantha Daniel. Amber's sister."

17.

Barrett Thomas laughed. "I haven't heard that psycho's name in a long time."

"You wanna tell us about Samantha Daniel?" Miguel continued the questioning with Daphne's new information.

Barrett shrugged again. "There's nothing to tell. She was crazy. Case closed."

Miguel shook his head. "No. No, case not closed. Did she pay you? How did she get you to murder Amber?"

"Get me to? Like she was my boss? I don't think so." Barrett puffed out his chest.

"He doesn't even know." Daphne spoke the words as the realization dawned. "He's not lying. He has no idea he played into her hands."

"Listen, lady." Barrett leaned in, resting his muscular arms on the metal table he was chained to. "I don't play into anyone's hands. Samantha was just a lunatic who was obsessed with me."

"The night you beat Amber to death. What were you arguing about?" Miguel asked Barrett.

"Amber and I fought all the time. Am I supposed to remember one night? And I never killed nobody. That much I can tell you for sure." Barrett leaned back in his seat and again puffed his chest out to seem even larger than he already was.

Daphne dug in his thoughts, though she hated to do it, and watched the night unfold from his eyes. "Jealousy. He was mad about the other boyfriends."

"Which ones?" Miguel asked.

Daphne shrugged. "All of them." Before Miguel could ask how Barrett knew about all the boyfriends, Daphne offered, "Samantha filled him in because she knew he'd get mad. Worst case he just beats up someone she hated. Best case, he kills her."

"She wasn't dead when I left. I know that for a fact. Messed up? Sure. I knew we were never going to date again. But not dead. Not even unconscious." In this way Barrett again denied any involvement in Amber's death.

Daphne let out a big breath of air. "Also true. Amber thought he was her murderer because it was the last thing she remembered before she died." She turned to the large man across the table from her and raised her voice. "And he *is* guilty of assault with a deadly weapon." She turned back to Miguel. "But he didn't kill her."

"Samantha?" Miguel asked.

Daphne nodded.

Barrett laughed again from across the table. "I told you. She's a nut job. Amber was pretty good about keeping her secrets. Hell, I believed her when she said she wanted to marry me. But because her psycho sister was obsessed with her, she somehow found out about us and then came after me."

"What do you mean by 'came after you'?" Miguel

asked.

"She wanted my body." Barrett winked at Miguel.

"I was right when I was feeling jealousy originally. He was jealous of Amber's other boyfriends." Daphne indicated the inmate across the table. "And Samantha was jealous of Amber. Everything Amber had Samantha thought was to spite her somehow."

"So, how did it go from a couple of jealous people to a vicious attack and a homicide?" Miguel asked.

"This guy was easy to push over the edge. And Samantha knew it. He may have thought of her as just a psycho, but she knew every detail about him. In a twisted way, she loved him," Daphne explained. "She knew he was a powder keg of anger and destruction. She just had to light the match."

"So Barrett here confronts Amber about the boyfriends and it goes south," Miguel reiterated. "How does she end up dead?"

"After he left the scene, one person stayed,"

Daphne answered. Miguel noticed she was looking over his shoulder. He turned to follow her gaze but nothing was there.

"Amber. She's learning the truth today, too," Daphne explained. The ghost of Melissa Amber Daniel stood in the corner, eyes wide with the horror of two people she'd cared about betraying her so completely.

"Call Victoria," Daphne instructed Miguel. "Get the official cause of death."

"I haven't looked into his face since the night he beat me and left me for dead," Amber said. Daphne could feel her emotions and they were laced with sadness and disappointment. Daphne expected anger at the injustice—wanted Amber to be angry even—but anger wasn't present. "He's very different," Amber added.

"Well, he's gotten older," Daphne said, shrugging.

Miguel ignored her talking to ghosts as he called the Medical Examiner's office.

But Amber shook her head. "Not that. He's harder. Colder. The Barrett I knew must've had that hardness buried very deep, because he was gentle with me. Until that day." Amber looked at Barrett, the man she would've run away with. She had a haunted look that went beyond just being a ghost. "Samantha took so much from the both of us."

"What's happening right now?" Barrett was astute enough to know that Daphne's conversation with the thin air meant something, even if he wasn't sure what.

"Amber isn't mad at you, even though she should be. She feels like Samantha took both your lives that day," Daphne explained.

"That's nonsense," Barrett responded, but his voice and face didn't reflect his words.

"You know I'm right." Daphne turned back toward Barrett, sensing the truth as she spoke to him. "She's haunted you for years, and not just her memory."

"Don't be ridiculous." Barrett again denied Daphne's words, but Daphne felt that his denial was empty and bleak.

"That was her." Daphne looked deep into his eyes. She didn't need to dig back through memories because this fact was sitting there on top like cold foam on the top of a coffee drink. It was just waiting to be scooped right up and served on a spoon. "The guilt you felt for all those years turned you into the very person you were trying so hard not to be. But she was with you. And she's not even mad at you. She forgives you."

Miguel hung up and announced, "Throat slit. There were knife marks on the skeleton indicating a deep wound to the neck." He nodded at the tough guy across the table. "Looks like the fractures he inflicted weren't the only ones she faced that night."

"I never knew what happened to her." Barrett's shoulders slumped. For the first time since entering the room with the orange door he looked deflated. The weight of the whole event, his own mistakes compounded with forty years of not knowing Amber's fate had fortified into a statue of anger, hate and rage. But now the anger had changed to remorse. "That's the honest truth. I hate what I did to her. I hate myself for doing it. But I never wanted her to die. I never wanted that ghost to be Amber."

Barrett locked eyes with Daphne. His breath shuddered and his shoulders shook as the tears began to pool and fall from his eyes. And then he began to sob really loudly.

"What is happening right now?" Alanna had to ask. She was intrigued to come along on this fight for justice, but she was very confused at the turn of events.

"Amber may forgive him. Amber may not be angry." Daphne kept her eyes locked on Barrett as she gestured toward the ghost in the corner of the room. "But I am angry, and I think people should pay for what they've done. Especially when it leads to their death."

Barrett sobbed louder, covering his face with his hands.

Miguel looked at Alanna, who shrugged. And then at Anne Marie, who smirked. To Daphne, he said, "Well. He seems sorry now. Can we forgive him and go interview the real murderer?"

"Oh, this? This is me," Daphne explained with a shrug.

"What is you?" Miguel asked, looking between the sobbing oversized inmate and his quirky psychic fiancée.

"I took my mom's advice." Daphne jabbed a thumb at Alanna, standing against the wall behind her. "I used the emotions to help tell the story."

Alanna looked at Miguel and shrugged, clearly still not sure what exactly had transpired before her very eyes.

But Anne Marie began to laugh. It had been years since she had let herself feel so amused, and this made her laugh all the harder. From deep in her gut the laughter bellowed forth, loud and strong.

And then Daphne started laughing. And this made Miguel and Alanna have to laugh.

So, in between sobs, even Barrett let a few chuckles loose.

And in the corner of the room, the ghost of Amber Daniel smiled softly before she disappeared. She had made her peace with Barrett, and she knew her soul would soon be at rest.

18.

"I don't even know what just happened," Alanna announced when they were outside. "But seeing a big scary guy break down like that?" She shook her head. "That's real power, Daphne."

"I just did what you told me to do," Daphne explained.

"After all these years, you pick now to listen to me?" Alanna smiled playfully.

"Masterfully done, Daphne. I might even say I am a little jealous." Anne Marie put on her sunglasses as they stood there in the bright California sunshine. Her hair was up in a bun, or she was sure it would be matted to her neck. It had been some time since she was standing in the sun for any extended period of time. Standing in the sun with other people? Even less frequent. "It never occurred to me to give it right back to the perps. How freeing."

"So Daphne isn't surrounded by darkness?" Miguel asked.

"I'd still burn the candle to be safe." Anne Marie looked at Daphne. "Doesn't hurt, right? But you seem to have your own methods of dealing with things."

Daphne squinted as she looked between Miguel and Anne Marie. "That was a very weak mind. He had spent years toughening himself up physically but doing nothing to prepare himself for psychological warfare."

Anne Marie laughed again and the sound was shocking. Daphne could hardly remember another time Anne Marie had even smiled, let alone laughed. "Oh, Daphne. Thank you for letting me tag along. I can't remember ever having this much fun on a case."

"So what's next? We go track down Samantha Daniel?" Alanna asked. She saw no reason to dwell on Daphne's ability to make grown men cry.

"I'll have Gina and Sheffley track her down for

us." Miguel responded with a nod. "And we're going to need to find the murder weapon. If she confesses, it's something, but the D.A. is going to want evidence that ties her to the crime."

Daphne put a hand to her forehead to shield her eyes. "I can have her take us to the necklace. And the knife too."

Anne Marie sobered, the previous laughter completely gone from her face. "Be careful. *That* is the mind you need to protect yourself from. Sororicide is a special breed of hatred and murder."

Daphne nodded. "I've got the candle."

"The world is a better place with people like you in it, Daphne Winters," Anne Marie stated as she turned her back on the group and walked back to her car.

"Aren't you coming with us to confront Samantha?" Daphne asked her mentor.

"Hard pass." Anne Marie opened her car door, back still to Daphne. "Watching Barrett Thomas squirm was pure entertainment. Dealing with sickos is not as fun. Besides, you don't need me anymore." She turned back around to say, "You already know everything I know and then some. My work here is done."

"What? No. That's ridiculous." Daphne started walking toward Anne Marie. "I know barely anything."

"Daphne." The Anne Marie Daphne was familiar with was back. All hard lines, stern tones and strict face. Daphne froze in place to listen to the words of the person who had taught her so much. The only other person Daphne could think of who truly understood her world. Daphne hung on the next words from Anne Marie filled with anticipation. "You don't need me. And I'm retired."

The thought of begging, even grabbing a leg, crossed Daphne's mind as she watched Anne Marie climb in her car and start the engine. But then the feelings coming from Anne Marie were stronger, and Daphne knew she just needed peace. Earlier, Anne Marie had been driven by a curiosity that was now satiated.

There was nothing here for her anymore. So Daphne's arms fell to her side as she let her mentor go.

Anne Marie drove out of sight as the sun beat down on the parking lot.

"Daphne!" Miguel called out. He held up his phone when she turned back to her mother and fiancée. "It's Gina calling."

Miguel put the phone on speaker as Daphne walked back with heavy feet. And it wasn't just from her thick, black boots. "Go ahead, Gina. You're on speaker."

"Good," Gina responded through the phone. "And I'm here with Sheffley. How did it go with Barrett Thomas? Did he give us anything useful?"

Miguel looked at Daphne who rolled her eyes, so Miguel responded, "I'll say. We know who took the necklace. And persuaded Barrett to kill her."

"And then Daphne made him cry. It was so fun!" Alanna squealed into the phone. They could hear Gina and Sheffley laughing on the other side.

"I may have to find a lawyer to subpoena that footage for me," Gina responded through her laughs. "I'd really like to see that."

"So, you called us, Gina. What did you two discover?" Miguel ignored the diversion about crying Barrett.

"Victoria told us they've confirmed the remains are those of Melissa Amber Daniel. We wanted to notify the family before the press got a hold of it," Gina explained. "I hope you don't mind but we went ahead without you."

"Oh, man," Miguel answered. "We actually would've wanted to come along for that. You see, it's Amber's sister who masterminded the whole thing. We need to talk to her and Daphne needs to be in the room."

"Well, you aren't going to believe this one, then," Gina said with a cautionary tone. "But the sister's been missing for twenty years. The Daniels have just been assuming that both girls are dead."

"Samantha's not dead," Daphne announced flatly.

"Gina, why don't you start at the beginning? What happened with Amber's parents?" Miguel prodded.

"There's not much more to tell." Gina sighed. "Both parents were home, retired. They looked like they'd had a very hard life. Our news about Amber gave them a tiny ounce of relief, but they both looked like they had anvils tied around their necks."

"I can imagine," Miguel answered.

"When we don't have answers, our minds can go to dark places," Daphne added. With her serious face and her eyes squinting from the bright sun, she looked ominous there announcing the depths of despair we are all capable of sinking into.

"Exactly, Daphne," Gina said. "They had decided years ago that the worst had happened. They explained that they hadn't heard from Amber since the eighties, as we know.   And then eleven years later, Samantha disappeared. Sheffly pulled the missing persons report."

"Last seen August of 2001," Sheffley piped in, papers shuffling in the background as if to add credence to the existence of a missing persons claim. "She called out sick for work and was never seen again."

"Are the two cases related?" Gina had to ask.

Miguel looked at Daphne, who answered for the group. "Undoubtedly."

"So, she ran out of guilt? Eleven years later?" Gina asked, trying to wrap her mind around the bizarre situation.

"I highly doubt it was guilt. She must've had another scheme in mind. I don't know how I know, but I know she's alive," Daphne stated.

"Then it looks like we have to find her and ask her. She's the key to everything," Miguel said, eyes still locked with Daphne's.

"Agreed." Gina's voice came through the phone. "But we're right back at the beginning. We don't know the first place to look."

"But what if we don't have to look at all?" Daphne asked, shifting her focus from Miguel to her mother. Alanna just shrugged. "Maybe I'm not done taking a page from the Hollywood playbook."

"Am I supposed to know what that means?" Gina

asked with a laugh.

"It means that I have an idea of how we might be able to get Samantha to come to us." Daphne stared into the distance, face grim, hip cocked to the side—as if the very idea of what she had to do next was going to force her to do things she never thought possible.

But she had to do it, no matter how unpalatable the idea seemed. Because she knew from the depths of her soul that it would work.

19.

"What on earth could Daphne have up her sleeve, I wonder?" Sheffley asked as Gina hung up the phone and raised her feet onto her desk with a thud.

"Feet down, Malone!" The Sarge shouted from his office, without even standing up to confirm the noise was Gina with her feet on the desk.

Gina smiled before plopping her feet to the ground with another heavy thud. "If I had even an inkling of an idea about anything Daphne said or did, this case would already be closed."

"Do you really think Amber's sister masterminded her murder? That's awfully dark."

Gina placed a hand on Sheffley's shoulder. "Sometimes your newbie-ness is hard to miss." Gina shook her head and rolled her chair back to her own desk. "Yes. The more and more you handle these types of cases, the more and more you'll begin to see that anyone, anywhere is capable of anything."

"Wow, Gina. That's heavy." Sheffley turned back to the missing persons report, hoping something in it would jump off the page as a clue they could follow while they waited for Daphne to concoct her scheme.

"I know. It sounds jaded, but I prefer to think of it as an open mind." Gina typed her credentials into her computer. "You have to be open to wherever the evidence and clues take you, no matter what. That's what Miguel and I always did on Homicide."

"I guess that makes sense." Sheffley turned to his partner. "Hey, Gina. Let me ask you a question."

"Shoot."

"If Samantha Daniel wanted the necklace so bad, why didn't she just steal it? They were sisters. She could've taken it and run off at any time."

Gina shrugged. "The necklace may have been more of a sideshow than the main event. But it's hard to know for sure until the pieces all come together. Just remember, Sheffley, we don't have to prove motive. We have to prove murder. We always want to know why, but that's not what matters in court."

Sheffley nodded. "I guess so. It just feels like something is missing."

"That's good, Sheffley. Go with that. Instincts matter a lot in this job." Gina pointed at the young detective. "Now let me ask you something."

Sheffley looked up at Gina. "What?"

"What's your first name?"

They both laughed.

But after a short pause, he answered honestly, "Arthur."

Gina laughed. "That's not so bad. But I don't hear a single soul call you Arthur."

Sheffley shook his head. "Oh, I don't tell *anyone* my first name."

"Can I call you Artie?" Gina asked with a teasing smile. She tried to keep it light and playful, but truly she didn't think it was as bad as he made it out to be.

Sheffley huffed a laugh. "That's what my mom calls me. Artie James Sheffley. Junior."

"Ah, I get it. Gotta have some differentiation between junior and senior. I can see where that would be confusing under the same roof."

"Not under *my* roof." Sheffley looked away, pretending to be sifting through papers, even though his eyes were glossy and staring miles away from a single item on his desk. "So-called senior left before my first birthday. And *that's* my namesake?" Sheffley shook his head. "No, thank you."

Gina nodded. What could she say? Who would want to be named after the person who caused such pain. "Sheffley it is then. Screw Arthur!"

Sheffley gave her a sideways glance. "Yeah. Screw that guy."

"If we're swapping war stories." Gina leaned in. It was her curiosity that had caused Sheffley to open up about something painful in his life. It only felt fair that she share something, as well. After all, they were partners. And it hadn't been an easy road to get herself to the point of trusting—or even caring about—Sheffley in any capacity. "I was walking home from school one day, broad daylight. A group of guys pulled up in their lowrider and started heckling me. I ignored them and kept walking, which I guess only made them madder. So one of them got out and flashed his knife."

"Jesus!" Sheffley recoiled in horror on behalf of the young Gina. "How old were you?"

"High school." Gina frowned. "He grabbed me and pushed the knife up to my neck. You can see the small scar." She lifted her chin so Sheffley could lean in and get a look at the remnants of her wound. "And then they drove off. Just wanted to scare me more than anything, I guess."

"That's one way to do it," Sheffley muttered.

"But I don't hate that day. Do you know why?"

Sheffley shook his head in response. He would hate that day if he were her.

"I don't hate that day because it was the day, no, the *moment* when I decided to be a cop. I knew the millisecond that those guys drove away that I was going to make it my life's work to stop assholes like that." Gina folded her arms to accentuate her words.

"Okay, Detective Malone. I see your origin story." Sheffley nodded.

"And so, Arthur James Sheffley, Junior, maybe yours is also more than meets the eye," Gina explained. "Maybe being named after a jackass who abandoned you made you work twice as hard. Made you want to do everything in your power to *not* be like him."

Sheffley shoved Gina playfully. "Enough with the pep talk, Malone. I'm fine. And we have a murderer to find."

Gina pointed to the report in Sheffley's hand. "We know she's not actually missing. Her parents just don't know where she is."

"So what do we do next?" Sheffley asked. "How do we find her?"

"We start with the premise that somebody somewhere does, in fact, know where she is and who she really is even if she is using an alias," Gina explained. "I trust Daphne's methods will work, but there comes a point in preparing for trial when the prosecutor wants more than the psychic's honor."

"I wonder…" Sheffley trailed off in thought.

"What?" Gina asked, completely confused about where Sheffley was headed.

"Let's go chat with Spencer." Sheffley stood up. "I think I may have an idea."

"Okay," Gina agreed but still questioned where this was all going. She was still learning Sheffley and his approaches to things, although she had to admit deep inside that he had a lot more promise than she had originally given him credit for. "What are you thinking?"

"Social media." Sheffley grinned and wiggled his eyebrows and then started walking toward the room in back where the technical team was stationed.

"Uh, Sheffley. She went missing before social

media was a thing," Gina pointed out as she followed her partner.

"Yes, but as you said, she's only missing to her parents." Sheffley kept marching forward as he spoke without turning around.

Realization dawned on Gina. "Sheffley, that's genius! If we can find her alias, we can find her."

"And likely all her friends, and where she hangs out, her employer." Sheffley shook his head. "Honestly, people who commit crimes probably post too much."

Gina snorted. "Probably everyone posts too much."

"Spencer!" Sheffley called as he walked into the room. All the lights were off, as if the contrast between the computer screens and the dark tech room were the only things that kept all the techs from going blind.

In response, a young man with disheveled hair and a dirty white T-shirt rolled his chair away from a large computer monitor. "That's me."

Gina had to shake her head at the sight of their

favorite tech. He had deep, dark circles under his eyes and stubble on his chin that had to be going on at least a couple of days. "Spence. You look terrible. Big case?"

"Yeah. Working on a husband-and-wife homicide where nothing in the house was taken except a thumb drive. Perp ransacked the whole place but left cash, diamonds, electronics. Just wanted what was on that drive."

Gina couldn't help herself. The old job lured her in and her curiosity took over. "So it was a hit. Sounds like they had evidence of something."

"What?" Sheffley looked back and forth between Spencer and Gina. "What did they know?"

Spencer took a hand and rubbed his face dramatically. The lack of sleep was finally catching up to him and he had to rub his face to remind himself it was still there. The code on his screen and his distorted thoughts had begun to be like the Matrix, where he wasn't sure if maybe he had taken the red pill after all. "That, my friend, is the very mystery I have been up all night trying to crack."

"Well, definitely keep us up to date on this case. Sounds fascinating," Gina told Spencer. "Who's lead detective?"

"Eddie Ball."

Gina nodded and pursed her lips. She had worked with him for a brief time before being forced into training Sheffley. He was all right. Just a little cocky for Gina's taste and didn't treat her as much of a partner. She always suspected that he hated having to work for a woman. If he caught a whiff of her asking about his case, he'd lose his mind.

"Can you spare some time from that case to help us find someone's social media profile?" Gina asked Spencer.

"Gladly. I could use the break to work on something simple. Who are we looking for?" Spencer rolled his chair back to his desk and placed his fingers just a breath above his keyboard, prepared to type away the moment he had a name.

"Well, we don't know for sure," Sheffley said. "Her real name is Samantha Daniel. But we suspect she is living under an alias now."

"And we don't know where," Gina added with a frown. She expected Spencer to turn around and tell her she was nuts for even asking.

But he didn't.

He just shrugged and said, "I'll look for emails, usernames and passwords for Samantha Daniel and see what I can cross-reference to any other accounts. Not as easy as I thought, but not the biggest challenge of my life."

Sheffley beamed as he looked at Gina. And she had to admit, she was feeling proud of her young protégé. He was catching on quickly, now that he had set aside his need to overcompensate.

Gina placed a hand on Spencer's shoulder and squeezed. "You're the best, Spence."

Without looking up, Spencer typed away feverishly and said, "That's what they all tell me."

"But I do recommend a shower break at some point today," Gina added, with a pat to Spencer's back.

"Showers are for wimps," Spencer responded without skipping a beat.

Sheffley turned horrified eyes to Gina, but she just laughed. This was just Spencer being Spencer.

They turned and began walking out of the dark tech room.

"I say we look for a record for Samantha Daniel and see if we can pin her down on any other crimes. I mean, if she's a murderer, she's not going to shy away from breaking the law…" Gina trailed off and stared at Sheffley.

He was frozen just outside the tech room, eyes wide open.

"Sheffley?" Gina asked, concerned for his mental health.

"Shh. I don't want her to leave," Sheffley stated cryptically.

But Gina followed his line of sight and saw

nothing there but filing cabinets. "Sheffley? Are you okay?"

"She's here," he whispered. "I can see her."

Gina stared at the empty space in front of her, willing the manifestation into sight. It didn't work. She was completely at a loss. "Who are we talking about?"

"The ghost. Amber."

She knew it was irrational, but Gina felt jealousy creeping up her body and heading toward her heart and mind. "Why is she appearing to you?"

Sheffley shrugged. "I guess I'm more sensitive than you." Last time he had seen a ghost was on their previous case and it had scared him right out of his wits. But seeing Daphne be so nonchalant had definitely fueled his progress toward acceptance.

But Gina just grunted in response to that. No way was Sheffley more sensitive than her. And she had been open-minded from the moment of Daphne's entrance. She chose to swallow her feelings of unfairness and use this moment to their advantage. "Ask her about her sister."

Sheffley shook his head. "I don't know if I can. No ghosts have ever talked to me."

"Just ask her." Gina gave his arm a gentle shove of encouragement.

Sheffley cleared his throat and stared at his feet as a uniformed officer walked by, sparing a side eye at Gina and Sheffley whispering in front of filing cabinets. He absolutely did not want his co-workers to see him talking to a ghost.

Gina watched the officer, and when she knew he was out of earshot, she shoved Sheffley again. "Go on."

"Uh," Sheffley began. He could feel his face getting hot at the discomfort he felt at this. Daphne had made it look so easy. "It would really help us if we could find Samantha. Do you know where she is?"

Amber Daniel stood there staring back at Sheffley with empty eyes. Her almost translucent body was frozen in time back in the eighties and it made Sheffley sad to see. The visual manifestation reminded him painfully of the fact that her life had been cut short by her own sister's evil. He was about to ask again when she began to fade away until there was nothing left.

Sheffley shook his head, suddenly afraid that maybe he'd never seen anything at all and he was losing his mind. Did he actually think he was becoming psychic like Daphne? What an idiot.

"What did she say?" Gina prodded.

"She's gone." Sheffley said with a frown.

"She didn't answer? Shit."

As if in punctuation of Gina's disappointment, the top drawer of the filing cabinet flew open and papers started flying out one by one. It looked like they were being shot out of a cannon.

Frantically, Sheffley and Gina began trying to catch the papers in vain. Maybe a paper or two would land in their hands, but mostly they were scattering to the floor.

"What the hell is all this?" The Sarge barked behind them.

As quickly as it had begun, the paper flying stopped and Gina and Sheffley were left standing there in front of their boss surrounded by papers strewn all over the floor. And there was no explanation, not one that they could share anyway.

"Oh. I tripped." It was the best that Gina could come up with.

The Sarge stared at her for a moment, deciding whether or not he wanted to believe her story before stating, "Clean this up. Now."

As he walked away, Gina released a sigh of relief.

But Sheffley nudged her with the hand that held a piece of paper, one of the few that he had actually caught. "Uh, Gina. You're going to want to take a look at this."

Gina pulled the paper out of Sheffley's hand and read it quickly, taking only a moment to realize that Amber had in fact answered Sheffley's question.

"Well, I'll be damned."

20.

"Are you actually ready for this?" Miguel asked Daphne as he rubbed circles in her lower back.

"Not at all," Daphne responded bluntly. She exhaled a heavy breath and rubbed her palms against her skirt.

"Just lift your chin and remember they are lucky to be in your presence." Alanna tried to smooth one of Daphne's stray hairs, but it immediately sprang back to its wayward position.

"Mom. You're not really helping." Daphne glared at her movie star mother, suddenly very envious of her comfort in front of a camera. Daphne had never thought about being in this position—never had wanted to be in this position—so she'd never even slightly wished for any of her mother's traits.

"Okay, Miguel and Daphne. Here are your talking points." Julia Monroe, the Fresno Police Department's public relations director, handed a piece of paper to Miguel, but when she turned to hand a copy to Daphne, Daphne shook her head.

"Don't need one."

At Julia's confused look, Miguel explained, "She's clairvoyant. She knows what you want her to say."

"Oh. Ummm." Julia dug through her own notes, looking for any advice on how to handle this situation. Finding absolutely nothing, she gave up and gestured to the microphones set up on a podium in front of the courthouse. "Well, it's time. If you keep the press waiting too long, they'll just make up stories about you."

Daphne snorted.

Alanna patted Daphne's shoulder. "You can use some good press, honey. People have short attention spans, so they will soon forget how you lost your mind in the viral video if you pull this off."

Daphne turned a look of doom to her mother, who smiled back large and bright. "Very motivational, Mom." Daphne rolled her eyes at her still smiling mother.

"Come on." Miguel walked up to the podium, hand in hand with Daphne. She walked with heavy feet but didn't pull back.

Miguel cleared his throat and adjusted one of the microphones to where it aligned with his mouth. Daphne stood slightly to the left of him, adjacent but as if she were a decoration and not the main display. "I'm Detective Miguel Alvarez, and I'm here with Daphne Winters, a consultant with the Fresno P.D." Cameras flashed and reporters leaned in, pencils in hand to hear what the police department may have to say. "We have information regarding a cold case from 1989. A young student named Melissa Amber Daniel went missing on her way to work at the Denny's on Shaw near First Street that night and never made it to work and was never seen again."

More flashes. More scribbles in notepads.

Daphne cringed at it all. She had to keep herself focused on the end goal of getting justice for the innocent victim Miguel was talking about. It wasn't Amber's fault she was pretty, charismatic and smart. And even if it was, it still wasn't reason enough to end her life. But if it weren't for her desire to pull Samantha Daniel out of hiding, no way would Daphne ever be standing in front of the press.

Their locust-style desire to devour everything in sight made Daphne's skin crawl.

"We cannot divulge too many details at this time." Miguel spoke the words from his public relations notes. "This is an ongoing and active investigation. But I can confirm that Miss Daniel's remains were discovered recently and positively ID'd. Her death was determined to be a homicide. We have reason to believe there may have been more than one person involved in Miss Daniel's death." Miguel turned to Daphne. "Ms.

Winters?"

Daphne took a deep breath and stepped forward, forcing Miguel to step back and out of the way. Daphne may not like the press but she could certainly use every tool to her advantage, just as she always had. "Miss Daniel's sister, Samantha Daniel, was there that night and is wanted for questioning." Daphne looked straight at the news camera rolling footage in front of her. "Samantha. This is your chance to come forward and tell your side of the story. I am sure there is a book deal in there for you." Daphne appealed to her vanity. "Maybe even morning talk shows and podcasts. This is your chance." And then she glanced at her mother, imagining another way to pull her out of hiding. "And there's a five-thousand-dollar reward for you if you come forward."

Alanna had the money to spare, so Daphne didn't feel too guilty for not asking first.

Miguel leaned over Daphne's shoulder. "We're happy to take any questions at this time."

A hyper gentleman in front, really overdressed

for the hot summer day, was waving his hand wildly at Miguel. Miguel had barely glanced in his direction when he began to ask, "You say that Samantha was there that night that her sister died, Miss Winters. What evidence do you have?"

"We cannot divulge details of the active investigation," Miguel stuck to the party line.

But Daphne wasn't a detective. "I'm psychic and I saw her. She watched the whole thing. And did nothing."

There were several gasps throughout the crowd of reporters, photographers and camera operators. Daphne knew some were for her declaration of her gift. But she told herself that a few might be because Samantha's behavior was so despicable.

"You mean to tell us that all of this is based on the word of a psychic?" another reporter shot out.

"So Samantha Daniel is just a witness?" someone else asked.

"Who killed Amber Daniel?" Another question

rang out. And then all the reporters started talking over one another.

"Listen, vultures." Daphne leaned into the microphone. "Samantha is involved and we need to find her. Are you going to help us or not?"

Her face was hot and her chest was heaving with emotion. And the reporters fell silent at the reverse question.

Miguel gently nudged Daphne to step away from the microphone and leaned in himself. "We have one person in custody who has already divulged several details I cannot get into at this time. We just want to talk to Samantha Daniel. As Miss Winters suggested, we are asking the help of the public to find her and encourage her to come forward. That is all at this time."

Miguel began walking away from the podium, assuming Daphne would follow. She didn't.

After standing there internally debating whether or not she should just walk away, Daphne decided she had one more thing to say. She waved her mother to the stage, and Alanna obliged, while Julia looked on in confusion mixed with a twinge of horror.

Julia was used to planning for all sorts of contingencies. But she hadn't counted on the wildcard that was Daphne Winters.

"I know what you're all thinking," Daphne began. A slight echo of feedback reverberated through the microphone. Cameras still clicked non-stop, but the inquisitive reporters had remained silent. They waited eagerly to see what ratings gold this quirky psychic with a movie star at her side might bring.

"This is my mother, Alanna Savage. I grew up watching the press fawn all over her, following her around invading her privacy, and then turning on her when she no longer served their agenda. So my trust of everyone in this crowd is as low as your trust of me." More camera clicks and flashes. "So I apologize for any previous misconduct I might have had."

There were some murmurs and giggles from the crowd of reporters. They had her number as much as she had theirs. "Okay, fine. Misconduct I actually did." Daphne snorted. "But this isn't about me or you. It's about Melissa Amber Daniel. A woman whose only crime was wanting to become a teacher and leave a rough life behind. Help us get her family justice so her soul can rest."

Daphne turned to leave but saw her mother waving and smiling flirtatiously at the reporters, especially the male reporters. So she leaned back into the microphone and said, "Now we're done."

With a pull of Alanna's arm, Daphne stormed away from the podium and joined Miguel where he stood near the glass entrance to the police headquarters. Julia stepped into her role and made sure everyone in the press knew where to direct future questions as she wrapped up the event.

"As press briefings go, that was definitely my strangest," Miguel announced to Daphne and Alanna.

"Mine too, although any press is good press. It's just about getting your name out there," Alanna stated confidently.

"Mom. We're not here for your career. It's about Amber." Daphne rolled her eyes and shook her head. "Oh. Gina and Sheffley are here. They have something they want to share."

Miguel looked around but didn't see his partners anywhere. "Where?"

"Well, they haven't exactly arrived yet. But they'll be parking any minute now," Daphne clarified.

"Any clue what they want to share?" Miguel squinted into the vibrant Fresno sun as he looked at Daphne.

Daphne concentrated, opening up her mind. "They found something. Actually, Amber showed them something." Daphne wagged a finger toward Miguel. "Maybe Sheffley is beginning to show some psychic tendencies. This is his second ghost sighting. He's very open-minded for a cop."

"What's that supposed to mean?" Miguel asked with a laugh, although he wasn't offended at all. He knew it had taken a lot for him to become as open as he was now.

Alanna leaned toward Miguel. "I think she is saying that there is a difference between cold, hard facts and the spiritual world."

"No." Daphne shook her head. "I wasn't saying that at all."

And Miguel laughed harder as Gina came up behind him with Sheffley at her side.

"You guys will never believe this," Gina announced.

"Sheffley saw Amber's ghost and she pointed you to some new piece of evidence?" Miguel raised an eyebrow. At Gina's crestfallen face, Miguel added, "Don't worry. Daphne didn't tell us what you found. That can still be your surprise."

"For some reason, it was buried in some old files in the cabinets near Tech." Sheffley held up the paper that had come their way with the help of Amber's ghost. "I'm starting to get your powers, Daphne."

Daphne folded her arms and leaned on one hip, but didn't dignify Sheffley's stupid statement with a response.

"Wow. I never even thought of that connection." Miguel held the paper for Daphne to read, and Alanna leaned over to see as well.

"I'm sure Daphne already sensed something," Alanna responded once she'd taken it all in.

Daphne snorted. "Well, I knew that guy was a piece of shit. I didn't realize how steaming, apparently."

21.

"Let me in." The hammering fist on his door was relentless. "I know you're in there, Dr. Kelly." More pounding. After all these years, and despite her own mature age, she would always call him by his professorial title.

"Go away. I don't want to be seen with you." Professor Stephen Kelly stood on the other side of the banging door, peering out the peephole window at the small girl who had entangled his life forever with Amber's.

Part of him now regretted not coming clean with the detectives and telling them everything.

He'd been honest. He had just been selective in his recounting, a fact he was grateful for once he knew they had brought along a psychic. Of course, he didn't believe in such nonsense, but he also couldn't afford to gamble wrong in his ignorance.

But really it was neither here nor there. He never wanted *anybody* to know his link to the missing woman. Correction—the murdered woman.

He never knew any details, of course, that much was true. But deep in his heart he knew the depravity of Samantha. If he'd ever allowed himself to ponder on it all, he would've instantly guessed Amber's fate. He buried his head to the truth of it all and pretended to have no connection all these years for good old-fashioned self-preservation.

"Open up, asshole!" The pounding was harder and the tone getting more aggressive. His wife, Pamela, had gone to the store but she wouldn't be gone forever. And she would surely have questions he couldn't answer if she came home and saw Samantha pounding on his front door. Well, questions he didn't want to answer.

He dug in his pocket for the detective's card—the card he swore to himself he'd never look at again. Only a few short days later and how his resolve had weakened. He texted the number on the card saying simply: *the person you are looking for is here.*

The response back from Detective Alvarez was swift and to the point: *Samantha?* So he responded in a similar curt manner: *Yes. Come to my house.*

And now he couldn't let her leave.

He had begun to spin the spider's web and he needed to keep his precious, murderous moth contained within. He just had to hope beyond any hope he had left that he himself wasn't devoured by this entanglement.

Professor Stephen Kelly opened the door.

Samantha Daniel stood before him with her red, swollen fist hanging midair. Her face was as puffy as her hand, like she'd banged it against his door as well a time or two. Or that she'd been crying. Or she was an alcoholic. Or, most likely of all, that all of the above were true.

"All right, all right. Come in and stop making a scene." Stephen Kelly ushered her in, making no disguise about looking behind her to see if any of his neighbors had noticed. When she was securely inside his home with no further prying eyes, he folded his arms and asked, "What do you want with me, Samantha?"

Samantha grinned, showing stained teeth to match her frazzled hair. She'd never been a great beauty like Amber, but she certainly wasn't ugly. If she had taken care of herself, she had all the ingredients to make a great life for herself. But that was not the route she had decided to take. The path she had chosen had just led her further and further away from society and any semblance of what would be called a good life. "Samantha. I haven't been called that in some time. I killed that name off not long after Amber. You would know all that if you'd ever answered my calls. I go by Leticia now."

Stephen could only shake his head. "What do you want?"

Samantha shrugged, as if she had come all this way and forced herself into Professor Kelly's home out of sheer boredom. "I think another hundred grand oughta do it."

Stephen reacted in horror before he could compose himself, the idea being so preposterous that after all these years she could be blackmailing him. Again. "I'm retired. I don't have it."

Samantha instantly switched from bored to aggressive, shouting in his face. "You think I'm an idiot? I've been tracking all your accounts for years. I know exactly how much you have. Don't lie to me anymore, Dr. Kelly."

It was clear in that moment that Stephen had let a very dangerous and unhinged person into his home. Her eyes were bulging and her face was flush. The young girl he knew once upon a time was gone, and she was replaced with a deranged witch. So Stephen played along. "Fine. A hundred grand. So you don't tell my wife? Or what's the deal this time?"

And she was back to bored, her shoulders slumping and her eyes popping back inside her head. It was scaring Stephen in a way he had rarely been scared before. "I was thinking maybe the press. After I tell your wife." Samantha sauntered over to the coffee table, slowly picking up each item from the centerpiece, inspecting it as if it were a rare jewel and then setting it back down. "You see, I saw that little stunt the Fresno P.D. pulled. It was everywhere. And *I'm* the person of interest?" She turned wild eyes back around to Stephen. "I guess they don't know that you're the one who got my sister pregnant."

Stephen recoiled from the words she spit at him, literally with spittle flying from her mouth. He hadn't heard them since Amber had said them—much more calmly, he might add—forty years ago. It had all been true that they'd had a terse discussion in the car that fateful day Amber went missing. And she had threatened to tell his wife. All true.

He had agreed to keep seeing Amber out of self-preservation. But he'd had no intention of keeping that child.

What he hadn't admitted, even to himself, was that Amber's disappearance was actually a great relief to him. The problem had made itself disappear.

And then Samantha showed up at his door demanding money or *she'd* tell his wife. He had had a moment of thinking these women were so vile. A family trait of blackmailing the men in their lives. But he had paid the money eagerly. He'd never had a second thought about throwing money at the problem to make it go away.

Amber gone. Samantha paid off.

His life was once again his own and he went back to his normal existence, pretending Amber had just been a story he had read about in the papers. Such a sad, sad tale, he would shake his head and say when the topic inevitably came up in social situations. He denied even to himself that they'd ever had more than a typical teacher-student relationship.

Let alone that he'd fathered a child that would never be born.

Not that he'd ever even given that a thought. Whether Amber was alive somewhere in hiding or dead, he knew the child's fate was the same.

"That's preposterous." Professor Kelly tried to be fervent in his denial, but his voice was weak. He knew he sounded guilty, so he stammered, "I don't know what you're talking about."

Samantha flopped down on his couch, her grimy hands touching everything and staining it with her germs and vile nature. He imagined the darkness in her soul seeping into the fibers and stubbornly refusing to ever wash out. He foolishly had a brief thought that his wife would find out about his past transgressions, not from the police or the newspapers, but from the shadow of evil now pouring into his couch.

"I have no idea what she ever saw in you." Samantha was inspecting a grubby fingernail as if it were some fine specimen and not the disgusting filth that it actually was. "You're a terrible liar." With a sudden jerkiness, she turned her head to Stephen and glared at him. Hard. "I wasted countless years on cons and counterfeiting when I could have been extorting money from you."

Samantha shook her head at the unfortunate mistake she'd made to follow one path of destruction instead of another.

"I'd prefer cash, but if you need to wire it again, I'll leave you with the banking instructions." Samantha shoved her hands to her knees, using the movement to stand up swiftly. "You have until Friday. Or I tell everyone."

It was his last desperate attempt. "No one will believe you." But even as he said the words, he knew they were feeble, sounding hollow and deceitful even to himself. Samantha didn't bother responding. Instead, she walked to Stephen and cupped his cheek with her grubby hand. It was course and gritty, rubbing his cheek painfully before he could pull away.

She put her hand on his door handle. "Friday. I'm a busy woman." And then she turned back around, speaking over her shoulder. "I've actually really missed you."

And then she opened the front door.

Daphne Winters stood on the other side of the door, arms folded across her chest, one hip cocked to the side. Behind her, Miguel, Gina and Sheffley hovered on the porch steps, slightly more surprised than Daphne that the door had opened without their knocking or ringing a doorbell.

"Hello, Samantha," Daphne said with a vicious smile. "Come for another payout, huh? Funds were drying up after all these decades?" Daphne shook her head. "Should've invested in social media, but who knew, right?"

Samantha tried to hide her shock, but she wasn't a very good actress. Her brow remained wrinkled as she stared at the crew before her. Miguel and Daphne she recognized from the press conference. It wasn't high level deductive reasoning to believe that Sheffley and Gina were also law enforcement of some kind.

"It's Leticia." Samantha cleared her throat and fidgeted with her clothes. The jig was up and she knew it, but she was arrogant enough to believe that she could talk her way out of this.

"It's Samantha!" Stephen stepped up behind her and pointed at her head. "She's been extorting money from me to keep me silent."

"Silent about what, I wonder?" Miguel asked.

"We're going to need you both to make statements," Gina added.

"And explain this in detail." Sheffley held the paper he'd found in the police files near Spencer's office area.

Stephen stepped forward to see but Samantha snatched it out of Sheffley's hands quickly. "That's nothing." And then she began ripping it to shreds.

Sheffley gasped at the destruction of his evidence.

"It *is* nothing," Daphne said turning to Sheffley, "because we won't need it when we have Professor

Kelly's statement." She turned back to Stephen. "His full statement this time."

Miguel shrugged. "And we can subpoena more bank records if we need them."

"Please. That's my wife's car." Professor Kelly pointed at a small Toyota pulling into the driveway. "Can we have this conversation somewhere else?"

"I think now is perfect." Daphne smiled. And then over her shoulder she shouted, "Mom! Can you please escort Mrs. Kelly into her living room?" And then Daphne shoved her way past Samantha and Stephen.

Stephen grabbed Daphne's wrist as she passed, terror and pleading in his eyes. His lies, betrayal and double life were about to be exposed. The shivering wild animal before her was nothing like the over-confident man they had investigated a few days ago.

Daphne shook free of his hold. "You either tell her or I will. And I won't be doing it to paint you in the best light."

"So, can I go?" Samantha asked, still standing in

front of the door. "You know what I did, apparently. What else do you need from me?"

"No, you may not leave." Miguel grabbed her arm and pulled her into the Kelly home. "You need to come clean now or this is going to end very badly. For both of you."

Gina and Sheffley filed in as well, hovering in the dark living room. The curtains were still drawn and all the lights were off. Stephen Kelly had been living in the shadows so long now that his home had become one, deep dark cave of secrets.

"Hi, everyone!" Alanna waved wildly with her right arm, her left arm linked with Pamela Kelly. "Allow me to introduce Pam." And then Alanna leaned forward and stage-whispered to Daphne. "She's actually a really big fan of mine."

"Mom." Daphne shook her head.

"The gang is all here. Start talking, Professor," Gina instructed.

He looked at his wife and swallowed hard. She

looked so frail and confused. Daphne actually felt somewhat sorry for the betrayed wife standing in the doorway. Her blonde hair dusted with gray, laugh lines accenting her eyes, but otherwise the woman before them was joyous in her ignorance. Pamela Kelly had lived a happy life, completely oblivious to the indiscretions of her husband.

But she had enough intuition to be worried now. Daphne could sense her trepidation, still clutching to the movie star who held her arm. "Stephen? What on earth is all this about?"

She looked around the room at all the unfamiliar faces.

"Yeah, Stephen." Daphne shoved his shoulder. "What is all this about?"

Stephen heaved a heavy sigh and sank in a nearby recliner, presumably the one he always sat it. His favorite chair. Daphne knew he'd sat in that chair on many a night, his smugness permeating the air as he pondered all the ways he'd gotten off scot-free.

"There was a young woman. A student of mine." Professor Kelly was staring at the floor, his hands clasped before him. "Her name was Melissa Amber Daniel. Amber. She went missing, presumed dead." He looked up at his wife, who watched him cautiously, terrified of what he would say next. There were so many possibilities from her perspective, and none of them were good. "She was a student of mine, but our relationship went beyond that of a teacher and student. It had grown...amorous."

"Oh, my God." Daphne looked at Miguel, complete shock on her face. "How did I not sense this before? Amber was pregnant with his child."

"What?" Miguel spoke aloud, but all the faces in the room except for Samantha and Stephen were plastered with utter shock.

Pamela finally broke from her stupor, but could only ask, "Stephen? Is this true?"

She dared him. Dared him to say it wasn't. Begged him with her eyes, the way she leaned forward away from Alanna and toward the man she had trusted with every aspect of her life.

Stephen could only nod, the words unable to form in his throat. The lies had turned to stone after all these years and were no longer malleable enough to form anything but a lump in his throat.

Pamela's knees went weak beneath her, and Alanna grabbed her to keep her steady, playing the role of steadfast friend to the woman whose life had just shattered before her very eyes in her very own dark living room.

And she didn't even need to call upon acting skills to remember what it felt like to learn of your husband's betrayal.

"All right, Samantha." Daphne turned to the wild-eyed woman who had remained eerily silent through the whole interchange between offensive husband and the wife he'd transgressed.

Samantha turned to Daphne and opened her mouth.

And then bolted out the front door.

22.

Miguel instantly turned to follow the murderous conspirator out the front door, but Daphne grabbed him and held him back.

"I got this," she said. And she stepped past the grieving wife and her own mother, momentarily blinded by the bright sun. She stepped casually out onto the front porch.

Stephen stood up from his favorite recliner. "Why is she going so slow? You can't let her get away. Samantha has been blackmailing me."

"We know. We saw the bank records, remember? Before they were shredded." Sheffley folded his arms, his angry tone allowing no doubt about how annoyed he was that Samantha had ripped up his precious find.

But Miguel just smiled. "She doesn't need to run. You'll see."

"Ick." Daphne couldn't help but gag at the prospect of digging into yet another twisted mind. So she made an impulse decision right there to do what she could without that. Instead, she closed her eyes and opened her mind to the driving forces of Samantha Daniel's life. What had driven her to hate her sister so much?

Images flashed in Daphne's mind. Two young girls, one so obviously their father's favorite. One child alone, neglected, jealousy building up inside of her for years. Two preteens, one outgoing and popular, the other friendless and sad. And the gap kept getting wider as they grew into teens and then young adults.

Samantha watched it all jealously from the sidelines.

"Samantha!" Daphne called out, but to no avail. Samantha continued running, turning between two houses on Professor Kelly's street. "Shit. I really don't want to have to run."

With a sigh, Daphne dug into Samantha's mind enough to make her feet stop moving. She felt instantly the emotional turmoil. Jealousy was definitely still stewing, but so was sadness, loneliness and even guilt. She actually felt bad about everything that had happened with her sister. Controlling Samantha, Daphne walked her back to in front of the Kelly home so that all Daphne had to do was walk to the edge of the grass.

The investigators and Professor Kelly watched from the doorstep. Alanna continued consoling Pamela inside the dark home.

"Samantha, listen to me. I was a lonely child too," Daphne explained, and as she spoke, she loosened her grip on Samantha's mind. She could sense that the girl was tired of running. And she was curious to discover she wasn't the only person in the world like her. "And I know things with your sister got out of control and you feel bad about that. But your parents deserve closure and quite honestly, so do you."

Samantha looked at Daphne with curious caution. She'd hoped this day would never come, but on the days she ever thought about it, she'd anticipated many things: interrogations, handcuffs, leading the cops to Amber's body.   Never understanding.   Never an ounce of compassion.

"Oh, you're going to jail, Samantha."   Daphne responded to her thoughts, but if Samantha was surprised by that, it didn't register any more than the entire conversation had. "Your obsession with your sister grew completely out of control. And yes, you deserved a fair chance at life, but it was never your sister's fault. She had no idea how it was making you feel. It definitely wasn't worthy of a death sentence."

"She never told anyone I existed. At Fresno State. Did you know that one? She just pretended I'd never been born!" Samantha's eyes welled up as she let the decades of emotion bubble over.

"Samantha."   Daphne sighed.   "You know perfectly well that Amber felt trapped too. She spent her days trying to escape your childhood just as you did. I can feel your guilt, so I know you know." Daphne walked closer and rubbed Samantha's arm. She had morphed from a lonely, spiteful child into a criminal mastermind, and somehow Daphne still felt sorry for her. "The funniest thing about it is, you and your sister both wanted the exact same thing. For her to be gone."

Samantha sobbed and fell to her knees, so without taking her eyes off the suspect, Daphne waved Miguel over. She wanted him to hear this.

"I hated her so much. Her perfect hair and her trendy clothes." Samantha laughed this weird strangled sound. "That dumb girly laugh that entranced all the boys. And teachers." She shot a dagger look toward Stephen Kelly. "When I saw my opening with Barrett, I took it. And I was happy when she was lifeless. I felt relieved." She looked up at Daphne with ringed eyes where her makeup had smudged from crying. "But it didn't take long for me to realize I had blamed her for everything and convinced myself that her death would set me free." She hung her head. "And I was so utterly wrong."

"You're a grown-ass woman. Time to take accountability. Stand up." And without using any tricks of the trade, Daphne was surprised that Samantha complied.

Miguel pulled out handcuffs and Samantha willingly gave him her wrists. "You are under arrest for the murder of Melissa Amber Daniel. You have the right to remain silent..."

Daphne stared down at Samantha while Miguel formally mirandized her. Samantha locked eyes with Daphne, the pent-up rage and jealousy sprinkled in with the relief that it was finally over.

"Is that...?" Daphne's question hung in the air as she noticed a lump in the front of Samantha's shirt. Without waiting for an answer, Daphne yanked the chain around Samantha's neck and a large diamond like the one Daphne had seen in her visions of Amber dangled before them all.

"Oooohhhh.   That *is* a fabulous necklace. Absolutely worth a mint," Alanna shouted out when she saw the stunning necklace they'd been talking about for days.

"Why were you asking me for money when you had that? You could've retired on the proceeds of selling that diamond." Professor Kelly was equally shocked when he saw the necklace's size and assumed its value.

"It was never for sale," Daphne explained to the group, sensing Samantha's rationale for keeping it all these years. Samantha was telegraphing her emotions without saying a word. "This necklace represented who she always wanted to be, tried to be as Letitia."

"I'll take it as evidence, Daphne." Gina came up behind the culprit and removed it from her neck.

"I've never taken it off.   All these years." Samantha fought back the regret that washed over her.

"I was lonely growing up too," Daphne said again, and Samantha turned her lips to an almost-smile. It was clear that she'd always needed someone like her. She'd needed someone who understood and could tell her she was not alone in this world. But it was too late now. That ship had long since sailed. "But you pissed everything away and took the most important thing in your life completely for granted."

Samantha cocked her head to the side as she debated all the options Daphne might be referring to.

Daphne smiled as she thought back on her childhood, idyllic in so many ways, yet ultimately isolating and lonely. She had money, famous parents, invites to Hollywood parties, homes in the hills overlooking the ocean. But, like Samantha, she was lacking in something she felt was foundational: someone who understood her.

She looked back at her mother, now watching from the doorway, still propping up a distraught Pamela Kelly.

"I would have done anything to have a sister."

23.

"I got her. She has five aliases. Letitia Johnson being the most recent." Spencer dropped the printouts onto the conference table in front of Gina and Sheffley. "I mean, this one, her first... I can't even believe people had a hard time finding her."

Gina picked up the document Spencer was gesturing to. "Sam Samuel. Yeah, pretty close to Sam Daniel."

"And it even sounds fake," Sheffley huffed. "Two names twice."

"Her effort in the beginning was pretty minimal," Spencer explained. "But then again, no one was looking for her then because they had no idea a crime had been committed. Only she and Barrett knew the truth at that point."

"And where did Barrett go right after the murder?" Gina was building a timeline in her mind that she could hand to the prosecution.

"Are you thinking of charging him?" Sheffley asked.

"Damn right I am." Gina was fuming. "He may not have killed her but without him Samantha wouldn't have been able to."

"He hightailed it out of there and changed his route to avoid Fresno," Spencer explained. "He was caught up in armed robbery, assault, a number of violent offenses. His life pretty much after that day was in and out of incarceration. But he never returned to the scene of the crime."

Gina shook her head. "Never even inquired what happened to the girlfriend he beat almost to death."

"Well, there is certainly enough evidence to charge Samantha. The bank statements Stephen Kelly provided. *After* Samantha ripped up my copies." It was clear Sheffley was still cranky about that. He shook his head in frustration.

"Victoria's autopsy report. Barrett's, Stephen's and even Samantha's statements," Spencer added. "Not to mention her five aliases and several acts of counterfeiting that I have the paper trail on."

Gina started gathering all the various pieces of evidence from the file into a large pile. "Oh, Samantha is going to jail for the rest of her life. The DA will likely stack on each individual charge so that she gets the maximum sentence for each. Murder, conspiracy, extortion, stalking…"

"And tampering with evidence and hindering a police investigation." Sheffley frowned. "I'm going to make sure they add that to the list. I'm really upset."

Spencer rolled his eyes. "We've noticed."

"What a waste. Samantha's jealousy ruined her life and Barrett's, and ended Amber's." Gina shook her head at the unnecessary outcome. So much negativity from the obsession with her sister.

"Don't forget Stephen and Pam Kelly," Sheffley added. "There's no way they stay married after this."

Gina shrugged. "That you never know. But doubtful she'll ever trust him the same way again."

"It's classic how Samantha came out of the woodwork to extort more money from Stephen and all." Spencer leaned back with a smug smile. "But we would have caught her anyway from her messy inability to fly under the radar. From her social footprint"—he gestured to the various aliases they'd found in the paperwork Gina held in her hand—"to her overwhelming greed, she was bound to slip up somewhere along the line."

"Do you think we have enough? For a conviction?" Sheffley asked Gina, his more tenured investigator. He had only been a part of a few cases that had been presented to the District Attorney's office.

"If the defense team doesn't get Samantha's own statement thrown out of court, then yes, I do."

"But?" Sheffley raised an eyebrow as he questioned the part of the sentence that Gina left unsaid.

Gina sighed. "Well, at this point we can get Samantha for a lot of juicy stuff. Like ripping up your evidence." She nodded to Sheffley. He smirked in return. "But we don't have much more than he-said-she-said to tie her to the murder."

"The murder weapon would be good." Spencer shook his head. Digging through people's digital footprint? He could do that all day long. But chasing down physical evidence? Not his thing. "I wonder where that thing went."

"But it was forty years ago. No jury could possibly expect that we'd actually still have a chance at finding that." Sheffley looked questioningly at Gina, begging her to mentor him in the ways of criminal justice.

And Gina smiled in return.

"I suspect you're both right. Finding it should be next to impossible." Gina leaned back in her chair, resting the file of evidence on her lap. "But in this case, we have Daphne."

"Daphne knows where the murder weapon is?"

Sheffley couldn't believe their luck. And he was also surprised he hadn't thought of it himself.

"Let's just say she's following up on a lead, in her own psychic way." Gina laughed softly to herself. There was no doubt Daphne added a dash of spice to their investigations they would never have had otherwise. When it had just been herself and Miguel chasing down murderers, they had had a very different approach to closing cases.

But she loved this side of Miguel. He was open-minded and carefree in a way he had never been before he met Daphne. She had changed his life for the absolute better.

She had changed all their lives. And Gina was thankful for it.

Sheffley leaned in and lowered his voice, despite the fact they were in a conference room where no one but the three of them could hear their conversation. "Why do I see ghosts? Do you think I'm psychic too?"

Gina sobered and actually mulled this question

over in her mind. Why *did* Sheffley keep seeing ghosts?

"I don't know. Truly. But whatever the reason, I hope you are grateful for the gift." Gina rested her hand gently on Sheffley's arm as he sat next to her. "You may not always have Daphne in your career. But you'll always have your own abilities and intuition. And sometimes, that's all you have to go on."

Before Sheffley could digest Gina's advice, Spencer added, "She's right, Artie. If you hadn't found that bank statement from Amber's ghost, Samantha and Professor Kelly might not have been so forthcoming with their stories."

"Hey!" Sheffley glared at Spencer and then turned to Gina. "You swore you'd never tell!"

Gina held her hands up to declare her innocence. "And I never would." She turned an accusing eye to Spencer.

And Spencer smiled and shrugged. "Sometimes I have down time in the lab and I do a little digging."

"On our own team?" Gina asked.

"If you've used any type of technology, don't expect to think anything is a secret."   Spencer was unapologetic with his ruffled hair and stained T-shirt.

"Well, I guess that much is true. None of us really do have any secrets."   Gina had to admit that since knowing Daphne, your every thought, emotion or belief was on display at all times.

"But don't ever call me that again, Spencer." Sheffley hid a slightly veiled threat behind his words, his eyes showing how deadly serious he was. And given he had at least fifty pounds on the scrawny tech wizard, they all knew who would win in a physical altercation.

Gina stood up, clutching the case file. "Now that that is cleared up, let's head over to the DA, shall we?"

Sheffley followed Gina as he asked, "But don't we need to wait for Daphne? To confirm she has the murder weapon?"

"Nah. When she has it, she and Miguel will meet us there."

"So she for sure knows where it is?" Sheffley was

still skeptical that the missing piece would just fall into place so easily, ensuring Samantha Daniel would finally pay for her crimes all these decades later.

"Another piece of advice, Sheffley." Gina kept walking, heading toward the front of the large glass building they worked in. "If Daphne says she knows something, believe her."

24.

The Daniel family home had a cheerful exterior, despite the darkness that hovered. There was no way to break the news to a family that one of their own was dead, let alone by the hands of another family member.

You could almost see the darkness waiting to descend and take the white and yellow paint and make it toxic. Waiting to shrivel up the beautiful colored flowers that adorned the front flowerbeds. Eager to pounce on the welcome sign and shatter its words of openness into a thousand pieces.

Daphne rolled her shoulders like an athlete preparing for competition.

She was excited to give Amber's spirit some much needed and painfully prolonged peace. And she was honored to give the Daniel family closure. But there was no mistake about it. This was going to be rough.

"Just tell them I forgive her," Amber's ghost told Daphne, sensing her hesitation and nervousness.

"I'm right behind you," Miguel told Daphne, resting his hand on the small of her back, oblivious to the ghost also accompanying them to the front porch.

"You can both chill," Daphne snapped, her nerves frayed but steeled into determination at the task at hand. She didn't need them distracting her. It may be uncomfortable to talk to the parents, but her obligation was to Amber. Always to the ghost first. The victim. "I know what I'm doing."

For his part, Miguel could only assume who Daphne was referring to when she said "both." But he thankfully didn't press further or react to her reaction. He was going to be there, silent if need be, or vocal if need be.

Miguel had learned through years of partnership with Gina that sometimes he was the right one to take the lead, and sometimes it was Gina. He never questioned that or let it wound his ego. It was just practical. And it was no different with Daphne.

She alone was the conduit to Amber. He saw his role as providing the official representation of law enforcement. The physical embodiment of a promise of justice, however painful it may be in this instance.

Daphne pressed the button by the front door and stepped back as the chime echoed through the house. Amber's ghost stood next to her, a silent but equal partner to the news they were bringing.

Amber had never hated her family or blamed them for anything. She knew they had done their best. She knew it now in death more clearly than ever when she'd been alive and growing up in this home. Daphne sensed that Amber now realized that she had just been selfish. Being spiteful about not having money. It was the eighties after all.

Amber had thought at the time that she'd been somehow wronged by this life, that she hadn't been affluent, choosing to see all the few ways she was deficient, instead of focusing on all the things that were abundant in her life. She'd never had the chance to tell her parents that she now knew she'd been misguided.

Until now.

The front door opened and Amber's ghost squeezed Daphne's hand in solidarity and anticipation. It felt like a pressure to Daphne, and she welcomed the gesture.

"Mrs. Daniel?" Daphne asked.

"Uh, yes." Mrs. Daniel looked all around Daphne as if the answer to her visit would be printed on a yard sign or something.

"I'm Daphne Winters, psychic consultant with the Fresno Police Department." Daphne indicated the man behind her. "And this is Detective Miguel Alvarez."

"Henry! Get out here!" Mrs. Daniel wasted no time in both believing Daphne and understanding the purpose of the visit, at least as far as Amber was concerned. She clasped her hands together. "You found my baby. I saw the news."

She was smiling, but it carried a weight of forty years. Daphne sensed peace and relief more than sadness. After all these years, they hadn't given up hope—never that—just accepted the reality that Amber was never coming home. Coming home alive, at least.

Daphne nodded just as an elderly gentleman walked up behind his wife. He had none of the happiness his wife was expressing, but Daphne could sense deep down that this was a man who buried his emotions, but they were there. He needed answers just as much as his wife did.

"She's here with me. In fact, she was instrumental in helping us find her body and get you answers after all these years. She's waited a long time for peace, just as you have," Daphne explained.

Again, no reaction to Daphne's psychic explanations.

Mrs. Daniel continued smiling softly as she said, "I can feel her."

"Did she…" Mr. Daniel hesitated, and then, "Did

she suffer at all?"

Daphne looked at Amber, who nodded that she wanted her parents to know the full truth. They deserved as much. "She was in an altercation with a man she'd been seeing and he did beat her. But that's not what killed her. She died quickly and is no longer in any pain."

"Tell them I'm sorry," Amber instructed Daphne.

"She wants you to know that she never had any blame or animosity toward either of you, she just wanted to escape the Central Valley and hurry to make a life of her own. That's how she got tangled with Barrett Thomas, her attacker. She knows now that it was silly. And she apologizes to both of you for any pain she caused."

"All these years. We've just wanted answers." Tears began to well in Mrs. Daniel's eyes. "We never thought anything but that she was a victim and we're not going to start blaming her now."

"We're both far too old for that nonsense," Mr. Daniel added gruffly.

Daphne gave a side glance to Amber's ghost standing beside her. And Amber nodded for her to continue.

"There's more." Daphne winced at the next part. She knew people could be weak and selfish. She knew that hatred and jealousy drove people to do horrible things. She'd been working on homicide cases long enough to know the darkest sides of humanity. That didn't make it any easier to tell these grieving parents what their other daughter had done. "Amber was left for dead that night, beaten by Barrett. He admits to that. But then he drove off and someone came up and ended her life."

For the sake of their mental health, Daphne decided to leave out gruesome details. Likely it would all come out in the news anyway.

"Someone had been watching and waiting. Someone who had wanted Amber gone for a long time." Daphne cleared her throat, the words about their other daughter's involvement getting tangled up in the lump that was forming.

But the Daniel parents had been living with this for a long time now, and the puzzle pieces began to come together in their minds. "Sammy," Mrs. Daniel whispered.

"Samantha," Henry Daniel stated gruffly, emotion catching in his voice. And then his shoulders slumped.

And Daphne confirmed, "Yes. Samantha. That's why she's been on the run all these years."

With a hand circling her husband's back, Mrs. Daniel stated through the tears, "We never wanted to say the words out loud, as if it would make it be true somehow. But we've always wondered. It was so weird and suspicious. But we couldn't fathom."

Mr. Daniel just shook his head, too overcome with emotion. Despite his big frame and gruff voice, he was just a person confronted with emotions he didn't know how to handle and hadn't processed all these years. His wife was more emotionally mature and was handling it better.

Daphne understood both sides. Emotions overwhelmed her all the time, and she knew how exhausting it was. But she also knew you had to deal with them or they would win. Every time.

"Tell them I forgive her and I'm ready to move on," Amber instructed Daphne.

"But Mr. and Mrs. Daniel, don't worry. Amber forgives her sister completely. She wants you to, as well." Daphne looked to her right at the ghost with the eighties hair standing next to her. She was soft now, her pain and sadness fading to peace.

"Forgive? What?" Mr. Daniel was rocked in another direction with so many big waves coming at him from all around. Jealousy. Betrayal. Loss. Truth. Forgiveness. These were big themes. Just one alone would send you stumbling backward, let alone all of them all at once.

Daphne smiled as best she could, the way she imagined Gina would if she were here. "In death, sometimes you get clarity you never had in life. Amber now sees the truth of her sister's pain and the hard life she's lived because of her actions."

"I wish things had been different. I wish she had talked to me," Amber explained. "But I don't blame her anymore. I just wanted the truth to be known and for my body to be buried properly."

"She's asking for a proper funeral. Can you do that for her?" Daphne asked the Daniels.

"What? Of course." It was clear the Daniels would be processing all the information from this conversation for some time. Mrs. Daniel asked, "How do we get her back?"

Daphne noticed Mrs. Daniel carefully skirted the word "body" in asking for her daughter's remains.

Miguel stepped forward and said over Daphne's shoulders, "She's with the coroner's office now, but she'll be released soon and their office will call you. You can begin making arrangements any time."

"I'm ready to go, Daphne. But can you do me one more favor?" Amber asked.

"Of course." Daphne could never say no to a ghost in need. The Daniels just watched in awe as Daphne spoke to their daughter's ghost right in front of them.

"Please swing by Maggie's place. She needs to hear the full story from someone official. I hate that she put her life on hold for me." Amber spoke the words, but Daphne could sense there was no hate in her heart. She was past all that.

And Daphne knew it was true. Maggie needed the truth perhaps as much as Amber's parents had. "You have my word."

Amber smiled. "Then I think you have it from here. Thank you, Daphne." And with a kiss to both parents, Amber's soul crossed over on a beam of light.

"Were you talking to Amber just now?" Mrs. Daniel was incredulous.

Daphne nodded. "Yes. But she's crossed over now. Her soul is at peace at long last."

"We never got to say good-bye." There was no

animosity in Mrs. Daniel's words, just the punctuation on the lack of closure.

Daphne took a chance and placed a gentle hand on Mrs. Daniel's arm. "And you never have to. She's connected to you in a spiritual way that will never be broken. Just speak to her whenever you want to. She'll be able to hear you. Even from Heaven."

"How does that work?" Mr. Daniel's gruff, emotional voice was back to its old forceful self.

Daphne shrugged. She could sense things, but she wasn't all-knowing. "Mysterious ways, and all that."

Miguel cleared his throat behind her. "Daphne. The other reason we're here."

"Oh, yeah." Daphne's tone changed to more detective and less psychic. "I need to come into your house."

"I'm sorry. What?" Mrs. Daniel even stopped crying at the abrupt change from her daughter's spirit crossing over to a strange psychic wanting to enter their home.

"I do have a warrant," Miguel clarified. "But we don't intend to ransack your home or anything. We know exactly where to go."

"Yeah, we need Samantha's old room." Daphne started to push past the couple but they didn't even budge.

"Samantha hasn't had a room in our house for decades," Mr. Daniel explained. "I doubt what you're looking for is here."

Daphne sighed loudly and dramatically. "Yes. You're using it like a little office or den now. I know. But her old nightstand is still there."

Miguel put a calming hand on her arm. "We'll be quick, Mr. and Mrs. Daniel, and then we'll be out of your hair."

Mrs. Daniel looked up at her husband even as she responded to Miguel. "Well, I suppose if you have a warrant."

Wordlessly, Mr. Daniel stepped aside.

Daphne wasted no time in pushing her way into

the home and unceremoniously marching down the hall to the right.

Miguel smiled apologetically. "She's very eager."

"I have no idea what on earth you could be searching for," Mrs. Daniel said with wide, tear-soaked eyes. Miguel felt compassion for the older woman before him. She had been too clueless to everything, like a woman living in her own little bubble and today it finally burst.

"Yep. It's here, Miguel!" Daphne called down the hall and Miguel immediately hustled to the room Daphne was standing in, bottom drawer of a small white nightstand left open.

Mr. and Mrs. Daniel followed and hovered in the doorway. Again, Mrs. Daniel asked, "What? What are you looking for in that old nightstand?"

"Thank goodness you guys are pack rats or this could have gone badly," Daphne said, rolling her eyes.

Miguel put on rubber gloves and pulled a small clear bag out of his pocket. "The murder weapon, Mrs.

Daniel." The drawer was filled with books and notebooks, the covers doodled with teen-aged musings and line art. Miguel started digging.

"Way at the bottom in the back," Daphne instructed.

And then Miguel felt something that wasn't like the books. It was hard and cylindrical. He pulled it out and held it up.

And then Mrs. Daniel screamed. She covered her mouth to hide her shock, and also possibly so she didn't throw up. This day had tested the limits of her emotional stamina.

"All this time, we've had that *thing* here?" Mr. Daniel gestured at the knife with a curled lip of disgust.

Miguel dropped the knife into the evidence bag. "Looks that way. She stashed it, extorted Professor Kelly and ran."

"Samantha did all that?" Mrs. Daniel asked, still overcome with shock and disbelief.

Mr. Daniel just shook his head. "She's no

daughter of ours. We lost both our daughters years ago." His gruff exterior was a shell of what it once was, shoulders slumped, physically weighed down by grief and emotional exhaustion.

But then something caught his eye. He lifted his head and squinted as he stared out the window. "What the hell is all that about?"

Daphne marched to the window and pulled the curtain back to see armies of reporters, news vans, camera equipment all adorning the front of the Daniel home. "Oh, we should have expected this. It's the press."

"But we have nothing to say to the press." If it were possible for Mrs. Daniel to look more horrified than before, she was now completely beside herself, her face perpetually exuding utter astonishment.

"If I've learned anything, Mrs. Daniel." Daphne turned back from the window and walked over to the woman standing aghast before her. "It's that you don't want anyone else to define your story. Use them or they'll use you first."

"We wanted answers, but we certainly never wanted to have to go on the offensive with reporters and such." Mr. Daniel was tired and pale. This was a couple who had been through the ringer, and the press wasn't adding anything but pressure to a hand grenade.

"Just tell the truth. No one could ask any more of you. I worked homicide for many years before moving to cold cases," Miguel explained. "And one thing I learned is the families of the murder victims are absolutely victims too."

"But one piece of advice, if I may," Daphne added. "Don't flip them off. That doesn't turn out well."

25.

"Just come with me and stop asking so many questions." Andrea Alvarez shook her head as she led Daphne out to the backyard.

"You don't hide your thoughts as well as you think you do. I know what you're up to." Daphne snorted. "I am just stunned into disbelief."

As they stepped into Miguel's backyard, Daphne saw exactly what she expected to see. The warmth of the sun filled the space, casting soft shadows across the grass. A makeshift altar stood at the back of the lawn up against the fence, an archway they had rushed to buy at a home goods store that morning. It was covered in tiny yellow flowers.

But it didn't stop there. A small handful of white folding chairs, adorned with similar yellow flowers, were lined up in front of the altar.

Miguel stood there with his father and—most surprising of all—both of Daphne's parents. "Dad?"

Beck Winters cocked an eyebrow. "Your mother told me I had to."

So she turned her overwhelming emotions of shock—and a tiny bit of horror—over to Miguel, her seemingly complicit fiancée. "Miguel?! You knew about this?"

Miguel laughed. "Not exactly. They told me I had to help them with a backyard project."

"Andrea and I talked about it and we realized that we were planning the wedding *we* wanted you to have," Alanna explained. She was dressed in a heavily beaded gold dress that looked wildly expensive and out of place in the simple backyard set-up. "We both know perfectly well that you want simple and quiet. No fanfare."

"No crowds." Mr. Alvarez added with a smile.

"And no press." Beck Winters nodded to the group.

Mrs. Alvarez really laughed at that. "Definitely no press. Perhaps for the rest of your life."

When everyone erupted in laughter, Daphne rolled her eyes. "Okay, okay. I get it. So what's the plan here?"

"We're ready if you are," Alanna responded with a warm smile.

"There's no preacher," Daphne countered.

"Your mother told me I had to do that too. I was ordained yesterday." Beck shook a Bible.

"You? Beck Winters? A minister?" Daphne huffed a laugh. "That oughtta roll some graves."

"It's only for the purposes of marrying you two. I don't intend to start a mega church or anything. I don't want to get struck by lightning." Beck just shook his head when Miguel's parents laughed at what they thought was his attempt at humor.

"As for your dress..." Alanna looked down at Daphne's current attire of cargo pants, black tank top and thick, black boots. "We could go buy you something, but

I wasn't sure if you wanted to go...traditional."

"You could wear my dress if you wanted to, *querida*. I saved it all these years but never had any daughters to pass it down to." Mrs. Alvarez smiled softly. "Well, no daughters of my own."

Daphne pointed at her new soon-to-be mother-in-law. "That. I don't want to freely give any money to the establishment. Especially bridal shops and their inflated price-gouging."

"That's what we thought you might say." Alanna gestured to the back of the house where a wedding dress was hanging in the window. "Go put it on."

Daphne didn't want to voice it out loud, but even with psychic abilities, she had no idea how to put on a wedding dress.

"I can help you," Mrs. Alvarez said, sensing or knowing that this was something she needed.

And then Miguel turned to Daphne, who had been strangely quiet through this whole thing. She knew he didn't care about the pomp and circumstance any more than she did. She could see it on his face that he would take her lead on how they responded to their family's surprise wedding. "Miguel. Is this what you want?"

Miguel cocked an eyebrow and smiled. "As if you need to ask."

Alanna clapped when Daphne turned on her heel and marched back into the Alvarez home to put on the dress.

She stood in the back bedroom and stared at the white lace dress on the hanger in the window. It was delicate. Pretty. Feminine. For once she felt feelings she couldn't articulate. Never in her wildest imaginations had she envisioned herself wearing one of these. Marriage wasn't for weird girls who had a better relationship with ghosts than with people. But Miguel had changed everything.

Soulmates.

The word itself was preposterous. As if souls had just been paired together before time began or something ludicrous like that. She shouldn't even believe it. But here she was, staring at the dress she would wear to marry her soulmate.

"It doesn't bite." Andrea Alvarez spoke softly from the doorway where she'd been watching Daphne freeze before the dress.

"I think it's too pretty for me." She wasn't upset about it, just stating the facts.

"Well, I'm not sure what the Emily Post guidelines are for psychics, but don't most ghost brides appear in dresses just like this? You'll be in your element." Mrs. Alvarez laughed and it softened Daphne's frozen state.

"Are you suggesting I am like a ghost bride?" Daphne smiled at the joke.

"No." Mrs. Alvarez marched forward and lowered the dress from the hanger. "I am suggesting that you are over-thinking things just like Miguel does. Now strip."

The instruction left no room for insubordination. Daphne stripped down and allowed her new mother-in-law to dress her in the lacey white gown. She kept her thick, black boots on to balance out the outfit and make sure a little piece of her was represented.

"And I have something perfect for you." Mrs. Alvarez left the room and returned a moment later with a necklace. "This was my grandmother's. I want you to have it. It suits you more than me anyway."

Daphne faced the mirror as Mrs. Alvarez clasped the necklace, adjusting it on Daphne's chest. The chain was dark. Daphne didn't recognize the material, but it felt gothic in its style. In the center was a large ruby, shining so bright it almost felt like it was pulsating.

So maybe she did look a little like a ghost bride. And she couldn't argue that maybe it was her style.

And she couldn't help but think of the necklace that had been the symbol of everything wrong between the Daniel sisters. One who had a life people envied yet still was unfulfilled. The other a misfit who just wanted what her sister had. Including the necklace that represented so much more than the large diamond it appeared to be.

She didn't think anyone would murder her for the gothic necklace hanging around her neck right now.

"Should I fix my hair?" Daphne and Mrs. Alvarez inspected the reflection in the mirror, with blonde spikes poking up in every direction. Half her hair leaned left and half went right, none with any order whatsoever.

"Nope. It's perfect." Mrs. Alvarez leaned in and kissed Daphne's forehead.

Daphne smoothed the front of her poofy wedding gown. "I guess this is as good as it gets. Shall we?"

"We shall." And Andrea hooked her arm through Daphne's and led her out to the backyard. But they had scarcely stepped into the vibrant backyard when Mrs. Alvarez pulled on Daphne. "Wait. One more thing!"

Daphne didn't know that her mother had also gone inside the Alvarez home, until she emerged with a candle.

"It seemed more you than a bouquet of flowers,"

Alanna smiled.

Daphne took it and recognized it immediately as the candle Anne Marie had given her, instructing her to light so that the darkness that would permeate her soul every time she crept into the mind of a murderer would remain at bay. She was willing to respect the advice of a mentor who had trailblazed the field of forensic psychology using her psychic skills, but Daphne had never felt threatened by the minds she had entered. They all seemed run-of-the-mill criminal. Just ordinary people who had twisted and turned down the darkest paths of life because of jealousy, fear, or hatred. But she saw no reason not to give it a try. It couldn't hurt. She'd seen enough in her lifetime to know that much.

Daphne ran a finger along the strange markings on the sides of the candle.

"Are you sure, Mom? I know you want a traditional wedding." Daphne looked at her mother, the woman who had always been focused on parties and glamour. Alanna Savage would never willingly throw a party that was so subdued.

Alanna leaned in with a wink. "I had one of those, remember? A big, beautiful traditional wedding with hundreds of people and expensive decorations. And the marriage was still a sham." She wrapped one arm around her daughter in a side hug. "The wedding is just an event. The marriage is what matters."

Daphne had never understood her mother and had definitely never respected her decisions or her life's priorities. But suddenly she felt a shift in their relationship, like maybe they both were starting to get one another in a way they never had before. And Daphne surprised herself when she side-hugged her mother right back.

"Somebody light this baby." Daphne held the candle up and Mrs. Alvarez laughed as she grabbed a lighter from where it rested near the barbeque and lit the candle in Daphne's hands. "Will you both give me away?"

Both the mothers looked surprised at the

prospect of anybody giving Daphne away, let alone her choosing them, but they were honored. For Daphne, it just made sense.   One mother represented her upbringing and her past, the other represented the life she would build with Miguel in the future.

Andrea and Alanna each grabbed an arm, Daphne's candle held tight between her two hands, resting gently near her waist, standing there in the middle of the patio in a tiny backyard gathering of only the closest family.

And Daphne locked eyes with Miguel, who stared back as if he were the winner of some great prize he couldn't believe he had won. Daphne couldn't believe that he felt that way since she knew very well she was no picnic. But she wouldn't argue because she was walking toward something she had always wanted.

Not marriage, but acceptance. She had often daydreamed about someone who could love her despite her quirks. And here was someone who loved her *because* of them. It was beyond expectations.

She took a step toward Miguel and their future together.

"Daphne! Oh, my God. There you are!" A voice came around the side of the house. "They told me you might be here. I've been looking everywhere."

Daphne stared at the man accompanying the voice in disbelief. Was she being punked? "Derek? What's going on?"

"Is Detective Cayman okay?" Miguel had to ask, equally as shocked at Derek Cayman's sudden arrival.

But Daphne knew. "No. He's not." She frowned as an image flashed in her mind of her former mentor and father figure lying in a hospital bed, a bloody bandage across his chest. "He's been shot."

Derek looked from Daphne to Miguel, pleading for both to listen and understand. "Yes, he was shot. He's been helping on cases here and there. Not much, just something to fill the time in his retirement. It's basically a paper-pushing job."

Daphne crossed her arms across her chest,

carefully shifting the candle to one side so as not to singe her wedding dress. "Paper-pushing jobs don't get you shot."

"Exactly." Derek held his hands out to Daphne. "My mother sent me to find you. She said you'd know who did it."

"Did your father see anything that might give us a clue what happened?" Miguel asked.

Derek shook his head. He didn't know. "My dad's unconscious."

Daphne blew out her mojo candle and said, "We're obviously going to go back with you and help."

"Please." It was all Derek could say. He swallowed hard and his face was ashen white. It was a miracle to Daphne he'd been able to drive to Central California without getting in a wreck, he was so distraught.

As he should be. Who could possibly want to shoot Cayman? But actually, Daphne knew when you had a record as good as his, the answer was lots of people.

"Daphne? We're about to get married. Can we finish the ceremony first, at least?" Miguel asked, gesturing to her dad standing silently watching the scene before him.

"Yes. I am needed back on the set. And I can drive you back myself," Beck said.

"Fine. Wedding first. Then Southern California." Daphne narrowed her eyes. She hated seeing anyone be shot, or stabbed, or choked. From the barrage of ghosts she'd met over the years, she'd seen it all. But when it was personal, it just upped the ante. "We're going to find who did this. And they're going to pay."

To be continued in Daphne Winters Psychic Investigation Series #5: *The Silencer*.